She could do this

All she had to do was remain in character. Be polite, say "hello" and act as if she wasn't, at this very moment and every moment, terrified of someone—especially *this* someone—finding out her secret.

Resigned, she slowly faced Britney's older brother. She couldn't deny Nick Coletti was good-looking with his wavy dark hair, bittersweet-chocolate eyes and Roman features. He wore a snug, dark blue Police Academy T-shirt and faded jeans; a tool belt hung low on his narrow hips.

Her neck heated as she realized that not long ago, she would've been all over him. Thank goodness those days, and the person she used to be, were both long gone.

Dear Reader,

This book came as a total surprise to me. I'd already written three stories set in fictional Serenity Springs, New York, featuring connected characters, and I honestly thought all the stories in that town had been told.

I was right. But I was wrong, too.

You see, in my previous book, *His Secret Agenda*, there's a short scene featuring a nondescript woman. A woman on the run from her powerful, abusive husband. A woman with secrets. A woman who lies as easily as she breathes and who'd do anything to keep her young son safe from the man who'd hurt him. A woman I had to write about.

But I knew Faith Lewis couldn't stay in Serenity Springs, so I said goodbye to the town I'd come to love and ventured east to another small town, this one on the coast of Maine, where Faith and her son could have a fresh start. Where she could learn to overcome her mistakes.

Although I hadn't planned on writing this story, I sure had a great time doing it. Faith and her hero, local cop Nick Coletti, don't have an easy time of things but once they earn their happily-ever-after, everything they went through to get there was worth it.

I hope you agree and enjoy Faith and Nick's story!

I love to hear from readers. Please visit my Web site, www.bethandrews.net, or write to me at P.O. Box 714, Bradford, PA 16701.

Beth Andrews

Do You Take This Cop?
Beth Andrews

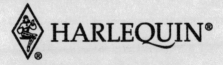

TORONTO • NEW YORK • LONDON
AMSTERDAM • PARIS • SYDNEY • HAMBURG
STOCKHOLM • ATHENS • TOKYO • MILAN • MADRID
PRAGUE • WARSAW • BUDAPEST • AUCKLAND

Recycling programs
for this product may
not exist in your area.

ISBN-13: 978-0-373-71634-0

DO YOU TAKE THIS COP?

Copyright © 2010 by Beth Burgoon.

www.eHarlequin.com

Printed in U.S.A.

ABOUT THE AUTHOR

Award-winning author Beth Andrews never fell for a cop while on the run but she did date her non-cop husband while attending cosmetology school. Though she only worked in a salon for a short time, she's kept up her stylist's skills over the years by cutting her bangs (always a mistake) and coloring her hair in a never-ending battle against grays. Beth also loves to bake and is currently obsessed with finding the perfect red velvet cake recipe. To learn more about Beth, her books or to check out some of her recipes, please visit her Web site, www.BethAndrews.net.

Books by Beth Andrews

HARLEQUIN SUPERROMANCE

1496—NOT WITHOUT HER FAMILY
1556—A NOT-SO-PERFECT PAST
1591—HIS SECRET AGENDA

PROLOGUE

NOT GUILTY.

The blood pounding in her ears, Lynne Addison stared blindly ahead as the judge thanked the jury and dismissed the case with a pound of his gavel. Lynne jumped, the sound echoing through her head.

At the table in front of her, her husband, Miles—the man she'd thought would make all of her dreams come true—gave his female defense attorney a hug before shaking his other attorney's hand.

"Oh, thank God," Sondra Wilkins said from the bench seat beside Lynne. Miles's secretary then stood and hurried over to congratulate her employer, the man she idolized so much she was willing to do anything for him.

Even destroy evidence and lie under oath.

The courtroom erupted with movement around Lynne as people collected their things and left to enjoy the rest of a warm spring afternoon. She forced herself to turn, to look over at the chubby, light-haired eleven-year-old boy across the aisle. He stood next to his distraught grandmother while she spoke to the two detectives who'd gathered the evidence against Miles.

Lynne had overheard one of the members of Miles's defense team remark on how unusual it was for a child—especially the accuser—to be present when the verdict was read. But she understood why the boy was here.

He'd wanted to see justice done.

At the bleak, dead look in his eyes, a primal scream rose in Lynne's throat. She dropped her gaze to her hands, twisted tightly together in her lap, and clamped her lips shut. Damn it, if that poor boy was strong enough to survive not only being sexually abused by someone he'd trusted, but also the horror of having to testify about the unspeakable things Miles had done to him, then by God, she'd be that strong, too.

She had to be. For her own son's sake.

Not guilty.

"Aren't you going to congratulate me?" Miles asked as he approached her, his blue eyes shining.

She curled her nails into her palms. From all outward appearances, Miles was perfect. Handsome. Successful. A man who shared his time and talents with those less fortunate. A successful businessman devoted to her and their young son, Jon.

"Lynne," he demanded in an undertone only she could hear as he kept his grin firmly in place, "I want you to congratulate me. Now."

Lynne got to her feet, her legs shaking, her stomach churning as she stepped into her husband's outstretched arms. She put her arms around him, her hands still fisted as he kissed the top of her head, his fingers digging painfully into her waist.

She shivered.

He stepped away, a look of concern on his face. For the people around them. "Honey, are you all right?"

"Actually…" She cleared her throat. "I'm not feeling very well."

"Can I get you a glass of water?" Allison Martin, the head of Miles's legal team, asked.

"No. Thank you. I…I think it's all just…catching up with me," she said weakly. "If you'll excuse me, I'll just take a moment to…freshen up."

"Let me walk you to the restroom," Miles said, touching her arm. She forced herself not to shrink from him.

"That's not necessary. Why don't I meet you in the car?" Before he could answer, she walked away, making sure to keep her movements unhurried as she went out into the wide hallway.

Inside the ladies' room, she rushed into the last stall, not even able to latch the door before nausea overcame her. Falling to her knees in front of the toilet, she retched, emptying the meager contents of her stomach. When she was done she flushed and, trembling from head to toe, got to her feet and stumbled out. Gripping the edges of a sink, she looked at her reflection in the mirror.

Her hair fell past her shoulders, the professional highlights like strands of sunshine in the honey blond. Despite the sweat beading on her forehead her makeup was perfect, her sedate herringbone pencil skirt and matching fitted jacket were high quality, her shoes and bag worth more than most people made in a week. She looked exactly like what she was. A rich man's wife.

Just what she'd always wanted to be.

She washed her hands, then snatched a few paper towels from the dispenser and soaked them in cold water. Pressed them to her face, careful not to smudge her makeup. Miles wouldn't like that. Especially today.

He'd told everyone justice would prevail, that he'd be found innocent of the horrific charges leveled against him.

He'd been right and wrong. Because justice hadn't prevailed. The jury hadn't believed Miles had sexually abused that boy. They'd bought the defense's claim that these allegations were a last-ditch effort on the boy's mother's part to extort money from Miles. To the jury, to everyone in their circle, Miles was a saint who'd been railroaded by the system and a confused young boy. They saw him as the victim.

But Lynne knew the truth.

She tossed the paper towels into the garbage, then cupped her hands under the running water and brought them to her mouth, rinsing out the acrid taste. She'd had such high hopes that Miles would be punished, that he'd be sent to prison, and she and Jon would finally be able to escape him. Her control shattering, she slid to the dirty floor.

Now they'd never be free.

CHAPTER ONE

Faith Lewis loved her son more than life itself. But honestly, if he whined at her one more time, she was going to duct tape his mouth shut.

"Why can't I stay home by myself?" Austin asked sullenly from the passenger seat. "I'm not a baby."

Then why are you acting like one? And worse, why had she reverted to thinking like a nine-year-old herself? She bit her tongue and strangled the steering wheel. If she'd learned one thing over the past twelve years, it was self-restraint.

Thank God she'd learned something, right?

She pulled into the municipal parking lot half a block down from Brit's Snips and shut off her car.

"It's not fair," he continued, crossing his arms, his green eyes shooting daggers at her. "I'm almost ten—"

"Last time I checked," she said, unbuckling her seat belt, "your birthday was eight months away."

He flipped back his brown hair. If he'd let her give him a trim, he wouldn't have to keep jerking his head like that.

"But *why* do I have to come to work with you?"

She pushed her sunglasses back on her head. "We've

talked about this before. So many times I might as well put it on a recording and push Play the next time you start in on me." And he would. Her son was nothing if not stubborn.

Like the color of his eyes, he got stubbornness from her. But that didn't make it any less frustrating. They'd had this conversation every day since school let out two weeks ago. It was going to be a very long summer.

"It's not like I'm gonna start the house on fire or something. Why can't I stay by myself?"

"For all the reasons I've already explained." Plus a few she'd kept to herself, such as her fear of coming home only to discover him gone. Tossing the keys in her purse, she opened the car door. "Now, I'm already late for work and you are about one more word away from losing your video-game privileges. Do you understand me?"

Scowling, Austin sank farther down into his seat. "Yeah," he muttered.

She raised an eyebrow—yes, just like her own mother used to do when Faith was little. This day kept getting worse. "Excuse me?"

"I mean, yes, ma'am."

Unlike her mother—who would've boxed her ears— Faith ignored the way he rolled his eyes. Hey, she didn't expect him to like having to toe the line. She'd done plenty of things in her life because she'd had to and not because she wanted to.

She stepped out into the bright sunshine, her light-weight shirt clinging to her skin. But that had more to do with her frantic morning than the unusual June heat wave, in the mid-eighties for three days straight.

Heat wave. If the people of Kingsville, Maine, thought this was hot, they should try spending a summer in a cramped trailer with no air-conditioning down in South Carolina.

It'd melt their Yankee brains.

"Run down to Reynolds' Mart," she said, handing Austin a ten dollar bill, "and buy yourself something for breakfast."

"Okay," he said eagerly.

"Don't even think of buying any boxed pastries, doughnuts and/or muffins. And avoid anything frosted, sprinkled with extra sugar, fried or carbonated."

His face fell. "What am I supposed to eat then?"

"How about some yogurt? And some fruit?"

Austin made a gagging noise. "Yogurt is gross. It's like eating cold snot."

Faith grimaced and slid her purse onto her shoulder. "Thank you for that visual."

"What if I got a breakfast sandwich? It's all healthy and stuff."

Sure it was. Eggs, cheese and sausage on a buttermilk biscuit. Her arteries hardened just thinking about it.

But the past had not only taught her self-restraint, it'd also taught her which battles were worth fighting. And wheeling and dealing with her son in the middle of downtown Kingsville wasn't one of them. Not when she was already two hours late for work.

"You can get the breakfast sandwich as long as you get some milk to go with it and a piece of fruit."

"You take the fun out of everything."

"Well, it is my sworn duty as your mother to make your life as miserable as possible. So glad to hear I'm doing a good job."

He rolled his eyes again but his lips quirked as he walked away.

She watched him as he went to the corner, looked both ways and crossed the street. A man in a dark business suit, his cell phone to his ear, approached Austin from the other direction. Faith clutched the strap of her purse. Austin, keeping his head down like she'd taught him, moved to the inside of the sidewalk and picked up his pace.

The man didn't give him a second glance. Exhaling, Faith put her sunglasses back on and walked off in the opposite direction. But she couldn't stop herself from glancing over her shoulder and checking on Austin.

Twice.

He needed to do things on his own, as much as feasibly possible, anyway. The store was only two blocks away. Austin was smart, responsible and more careful than a nine-year-old should ever have to be. And she'd chosen this coastal town as the place for their new lives because of the small town's quaintness and charm.

But mostly she'd chosen it because it was safe—and hopefully the last place anyone would think to look for them.

And yet she still wouldn't take a full breath until her son was back in her sight.

Fighting her natural instinct to keep to herself, Faith nodded and greeted people she passed as she hurried toward the salon. She knew how to play the game. All she had to do was be friendly. Normal. Act her part so the people in town wouldn't wonder. Wonder where she and Austin came from. Why they'd moved here four months ago.

Who they were.

Faith pushed open the door to Brit's Snips and stepped inside the air-conditioned building. The salon's owner, Britney Coletti, was at the back lowering a dryer over the tin-foiled head of a client. Removing her sunglasses, Faith's jaw dropped at the sight of her boss.

Britney had gone country today. She'd tamed her long, dark corkscrew curls into two fat braids. The low-cut brown vest and frayed micromini denim skirt showed ample amounts of her toned, tanned body. She leaned over to speak to her client and Faith winced and quickly averted her eyes. That flash of Brit's lady bits was more than Faith had ever wanted to see.

Faith tugged at the hem of her own baggy top. She wasn't a prude—far from it. Before she got married at the naive age of nineteen, her clothing had veered toward tight, skimpy and just this side of trashy. For the younger woman's sake, she just hoped a preference for tacky clothing was all Britney had in common with the person Faith used to be.

"I'm so sorry I'm late," Faith called over the low hum of the dryer. "Did Mrs. Willit mind rescheduling?"

"I got ahold of her and booked her for later in the

week." Britney grinned, her nose wrinkling adorably. "It's all good."

"Well, I appreciate you taking care of it. And I'll make it up to you somehow," Faith said as she went behind the counter and skimmed a finger down the appointment book. She still had fifteen minutes until her next appointment.

"Did you get ahold of the plumber?" Britney asked as she joined her.

"He's working over at that new motel outside town so he's busy until Friday." Faith tucked her hair behind her ear. She and Austin would be without hot water for a while yet. And she didn't even want to think about how much the plumber was going to charge.

She clutched the counter until the nausea passed. She'd brought this on herself by deciding to become a home owner rather than just renting a house. After all, what better way to hide than in plain sight? It'd taken her close to a year but she'd managed to save enough to buy her and Austin a whole new life, complete with birth certificates, social security cards and a credit history. It'd been worth every penny. By purchasing a house and becoming a full-fledged citizen of Kingsville, she was thumbing her nose at the people looking for her.

And proving she was ready to stay in one place longer than a few months.

"You can't live without hot water for that long," Britney exclaimed, as if Faith had admitted they'd be sleeping in the car a few nights. Which, sad to say, they'd had to do several times.

Faith hefted the strap of her bag over her shoulder. "It'll be fine."

Her stomach growled. When she'd gone down to her basement this morning to throw in a load of laundry, she'd been met with at least two inches of water. She hadn't had time for even a cup of coffee let alone anything to eat.

And while she might hand over a few dollars to feed her son, she wasn't about to waste money on herself. Especially since they'd have to buy lunch because she hadn't had time to pack it.

"I'm going to put my stuff away," she said. "If my ten o'clock gets here early, could you let me know?"

"Of course."

In the break room Faith tossed her bags on a chair and groaned as the unmistakable scent of coffee reached her. She headed straight to the coffeepot on the counter by the sink, but stumbled over something. She frowned down at a metal toolbox in the middle of the floor.

Hopping over the damn thing, she poured herself a cup of sanity.

Cup in hand, Faith stepped back over the toolbox and crossed to the mini fridge. Her choices were limited to half a ham-and-Swiss sandwich from yesterday or strawberry yogurt. Cold snot, hmm? She chose the sandwich.

As she chewed, the knots in her shoulders dissolved. At least the worst was over. It had to be. Her day couldn't possibly get any crappier.

She heard the back door open. "Hey, Faith." A familiar masculine voice. "How's it going?"

She viciously bit into her sandwich. There went her theory, blown all to bits. Guess she shouldn't have tempted fate.

All she had to do was remain in character. Be polite, say hello and act as if she wasn't, at this very moment and every moment, terrified of someone—especially *this* someone—finding out her secret. Resigned, she slowly faced Britney's older brother.

There was no denying Nick Coletti was good-looking. That is if you liked tall, broad-shouldered guys with wavy dark hair, bittersweet-chocolate-colored eyes and Roman features. Her tastes had always run toward men in designer suits over ones in snug T-shirts, faded jeans and a tool belt hanging low on narrow hips.

Too bad she'd also chosen men based on the size of their bank accounts instead of what kind of morals they had.

"I'm fine," she answered, sounding as prim as her husband's uptight secretary. "And you?"

He grinned, his teeth flashing white against his tanned skin. "Couldn't be better."

So what if his smile did funny things to her? All that proved was that she was female. She hung her head so her hair hid her face as she fought for composure. What made her a nervous wreck was that, instead of a tool belt, the man usually wore a holster and badge.

"Great," she mumbled, squeezing the sandwich out of shape. Reaching over to tear off a paper towel, she knocked the roll over. Nick caught it in one hand before it hit the floor.

"You sure you're okay?" he asked, handing it to her.

"You seem a bit—" her skin prickled under his scrutiny "—flustered."

Yes, he'd flustered her. How crazy was that? Used to be a time when *she* flustered men.

She ripped off a towel and wiped the mustard from her thumb. As long as she kept her cool, he'd never suspect he put her on edge. She set the towels back on the table and crushed the used one in her hand before rewrapping the rest of her sandwich and putting it back in the fridge.

And damn him for making her lose her appetite when she wouldn't have a chance to eat again for another three hours. "I've had a…hectic morning."

He nodded and twisted open a bottle of water. But even as he drank, his eyes didn't leave her. She calmly returned his gaze.

Let him stare. It wasn't as if he was interested in her. With her mousy hair and shapeless blue top and white, wide-legged cropped pants that made her curvy, hour-glass figure look at least ten pounds heavier, she hardly turned men's heads.

When she'd decided to become Faith Lewis, she'd ditched the colored contact lenses and fake glasses she'd used as a disguise for the past three years, but had kept the drab hair color and baggy clothes. It wasn't much but it made her feel safe. Even if she would rather shave off her eyebrows than wear another pair of mom jeans.

Sometimes you just had to suck it up and do whatever it took.

Because nothing, and no one, was going to destroy the life she and Austin were building in Kingsville.

NICK COULDN'T QUITE figure Faith out. She was pretty enough with her light green eyes and shoulder-length chestnut hair, but she sure was a jumpy thing. He'd gone out of his way to be friendly, not only because she worked for his sister but because she and her young son were new in town. But each time they ran into each other, she was as uneasy as the first time they'd met.

"I'd better go," she said, edging past him. No surprise there. She usually left a room as soon as he walked in.

Faith's escape was ruined, however, when she tripped on his toolbox.

He grabbed her to keep her from falling. Her body went rigid and she pulled away from him. "You all right?" he asked.

"Fine. I should've watched where I was going."

But when she took a step, he saw her wince. He crouched in front of her. "Did you twist your ankle?"

He raised his eyebrows as he noticed her shoes for the first time. High-heel wedged sandals with crisscross straps—the better to show the bright pink polish on her toes. They were girlie, sexy and totally inappropriate for someone who stood on her feet all day.

Nick touched her ankle to check for swelling. She inhaled sharply and sidestepped him. "I just stubbed my toe. Which wouldn't have happened," she said pointedly and, if he wasn't mistaken, irritably, "if you hadn't left your toolbox in the middle of the floor."

"You're right." He shoved it against the washing machine. "I ran out to my truck and wasn't thinking."

"You should be more careful." She helped herself to

more coffee. "If I can't work, I can't support my son—or help your sister build her business."

He straightened and shoved a hand through his hair. "Is that something they teach you at Mom School?"

"What are you talking about?"

"That." He gestured toward her. "The whole guilt thing."

She nodded slowly. "It's an advanced course for those who have passed Nagging 101 and the Art of Saying 'Because I Said So.'"

He fought a smile. He'd had no idea she could be such a smart-ass. "I've always suspected there was some sort of secret mom society."

"I'm sorry, but if I admit any more, they'll take away my membership."

And then she did something she'd never done before. At least not in front of him. She smiled. But it quickly faded.

"I have to go," she said, before walking away.

Faith Lewis sure was a puzzle. He tapped his fingers on top of the dryer. It seemed like ego, but most women were not in a hurry to get away from him. Damned if he couldn't resist a puzzle.

"How's Austin doing?" he asked, stopping her in her tracks. "He enjoying his summer?"

She took her time turning back to him. Something made it impossible for her to be rude enough to walk away when he was talking to her.

"Austin's fine," she said.

He leaned against the washing machine. "He's what? Ten?"

"Nine," she said, looking toward the door.

Yeah, he shouldn't enjoy this so much. But then again, he was a cop, not a saint. "I remember that age. Summer couldn't come soon enough, didn't last long enough and there was always too much to do."

"He's keeping busy."

"He making friends? Adjusting to the new town?"

"He's…shy. He wasn't in school long enough to buddy up with any of the kids, but I'm sure that'll change once it starts again."

"If you want, I could introduce him to a few of my nephews. I have one his age and—"

"That's not necessary."

"It's no big deal. And Trevor's a great kid."

"I'm sure he is but—"

"Mom!"

Faith's face went white. She whirled around as Austin came rushing into the room, his hair matted down with sweat, his face red.

"What happened?" Kneeling, she gripped his shoulder with her free hand. "What's wrong?"

The panic in her voice made Nick step forward, his heart picking up speed.

"The new X-Men comic is on sale," Austin panted, bending at the waist. "Can I get it? Please? It's only four dollars."

Faith sagged in relief. "The way you came barreling in here, yelling like that," she said, running an unsteady hand over her son's hair, "I thought something had happened to you."

"Sorry. I have to hurry back because there's only one copy left. Mr. Silvis said he'd hold on to it for me as long as I came back before lunchtime."

Faith rubbed her temples. "Mr. Silvis is just going to have to wait a few minutes. I hope you didn't run through the salon—"

"No, ma'am," Austin said, with such a guilty look Nick knew for damn sure Austin had barreled through the place as though his ass were on fire.

"And," Faith continued, "I can't help but wonder if you left your manners back at Mr. Silvis's store, since you haven't even said hello to Mr. Coletti."

"But, Mom, I have to—"

Faith gave him The Look. A shiver crept up Nick's spine even though The Look hadn't even been aimed at him. But it was a powerful tool, one perfected by mothers throughout the centuries to keep their kids in line. Hell, his mother had given him The Look last week. You couldn't outgrow it.

"Hi, Mr. Coletti," Austin said quickly. Nick nodded in greeting and Austin whipped around to face his mother again. "So? Can I get it? Please?"

"We'll see."

Austin's expression darkened. "That means no."

"It doesn't mean no. It means I'll think about it."

"Why can't you tell me now? Please, Mom. Please, I really want this one. And I promise, I won't ask for anything the rest of the week. Or even the rest of the summer. Or you could take it out of my birthday present or…or I could pay you back. Maybe I could mow Mrs. Sugden's yard again or walk her dog or—"

"Austin," Faith snapped, glancing at Nick before leading Austin over to the corner.

Nick didn't even bother pretending he wasn't observing their every move. Watching her collect herself was so fascinating.

"I'm sorry, honey," she said, "but with the water heater breaking, a comic book's not in the budget this week."

The poor kid sort of…deflated. As crushed as if someone had sold his prized baseball card collection at a garage sale for a quarter of its value.

Like Nick's sister Kathleen had done during his first year at college.

"Yes, ma'am," Austin murmured, blinking fiercely.

Nick clenched his hands. *Not his concern,* he assured himself as he shut off the water to the washing machine. Or his business. Faith had been distant around him since they'd met. No sense making waves with his sister's employee by sticking his nose where it didn't belong.

Austin sniffed and Nick tipped his head back and exhaled.

He was going to have to help the kid out, after all.

CHAPTER TWO

FAITH HAD BEEN GEARING UP for Austin to give her a hefty dose of snark about not being able to get the comic book, and instead, her baby had taken the news in stride.

"I'm sorry, honey," she said, deliberately ignoring the dark, silent man in the room. She brushed Austin's hair off his forehead, but let her hand drop when he jerked away. "Maybe you can get the next issue."

Austin shrugged. "Yeah. Sure."

"Damn," Nick muttered.

She and Austin both turned and saw him staring at his toolbox, his hands on his hips.

"Sorry," he said when he caught them watching. "I just realized I don't have any quarter inch pan head screws and…" He scratched his ear. "Hey, Austin, maybe you could do me a favor?"

"That depends on what it is," Faith said.

"I need those screws but I'm already behind fixing this…" He jerked a thumb at the washing machine. "Could you run down to the hardware store and pick them up for me? If it's all right with your mom."

Austin looked at her. The back of her neck prickled.

"But isn't the hardware store at the end of Main Street?" she asked.

"Yeah. At the corner of Kennedy and Main."

Six blocks away. Even if Austin ran there and back, he'd be gone at least twenty minutes. More than likely, with the way he ambled along, he'd be gone over half an hour. Anything could happen to him in that time.

In the act of pulling his wallet out of his back pocket, Nick paused. "If you don't want him crossing the street…"

"I can cross by myself," Austin said with all the offended pride someone under double digits could muster. "Can I, Mom? It's not like I have anything else to do, anyway."

She was stuck. Stuck between not wanting her son to do something as innocuous as walking down the street, and the cop looking at her as if she was a few rods short of a perm. "I…I suppose it's okay."

"I appreciate it." Nick handed Austin a ten dollar bill. "A hundred of them should be less than five dollars, so why don't you keep the other five?"

Faith stiffened and edged around so that she stood between him and Austin. "That's not nec—"

"I insist." Nick's eyes on hers were steady, his expression innocent. "He's doing me a favor and he should be compensated for it."

Austin tugged on her arm. "Can I, Mom? Please?"

Why did he have to look so excited? So…hopeful?

Worse, why did she have to feel so guilty? She got no enjoyment out of denying her child something as small as a comic book, especially after she'd grown up going without so many things.

"Did you eat your breakfast?" she asked.

Austin nodded vigorously. "I even ate a banana."

She forced a smile, surprised her face didn't crack. "Well, then, I guess it's okay."

"Really?" Austin asked breathlessly. "So, can I get the comic book?"

"It's your money. You can buy it if you want to."

"When you get to the store," Nick said, "tell Marsha I sent you. She'll have my order ready."

"Okay." Austin shoved the money into his pocket but didn't miss the way Faith raised an eyebrow at him. "I mean, yes, sir."

"I'll call her and let her know to expect you." He took his phone out and walked over to the washing machine as he dialed.

"Be careful crossing the street," Faith told Austin.

He squirmed in embarrassment. "Mo-om."

"Yes, I'm lame and overprotective and I've said all of this before. Humor me. Don't stop in any other stores besides the hardware store and bookstore and—"

"Don't talk to strangers. Don't get into the car with a stranger." He lowered his voice. "I'm not a baby."

"Maybe not, but you're still my baby." She supposed it was natural for a boy his age to be disgusted by someone calling him a baby. But that didn't mean she had to like his expression. "I just want you to be careful."

"I will be."

"I'll expect you back within thirty minutes," Faith said. "Got it?"

"Got it." He flicked a glance over his shoulder and, seeing Nick's back was turned, puckered his lips and accepted a quick peck from her.

"Don't run through the—"

Austin raced off. She prayed he wouldn't crash into anything in the salon. Such as a customer.

She dug through her purse and, as soon as Nick hung up his phone, stalked over to him. "Here."

Frowning at the five-dollar bill she held out, he stuck his phone in his front pocket. "What's this?"

"It's the money you paid my son to run an errand you didn't even need done."

His eyes were hooded, his expression blank. And to think at one time she used to be an expert on reading men. Either she'd lost her touch or he excelled at the whole stoic thing.

Probably the latter. After all, weren't all cops emotionless robots? The ones she'd dealt with were.

"I don't want your money, Faith."

Yeah? Well, she didn't want to give it to him, but more than that, she didn't want him to worm his way into her son's life with money. "Take it. Please," she insisted.

He held it as if it were a live rattlesnake before tossing it on top of the washing machine. "I'm not sure what the problem is."

"You stuck your nose into my personal business," she said before she could censor herself. "I'd prefer you didn't involve yourself in something that's between me and my son."

"I wasn't involving myself in anything," he said casually, as if he hadn't stepped over a line. "I needed some screws, he needed some cash."

She clasped her hands behind her back. "You're changing the hoses." Keeping her tone unfailingly polite just about killed her. "All you have to do is shut off the water, disconnect the hoses and connect the new ones."

"You moonlight as a plumber?"

She gritted her teeth. "It's not rocket science. Austin could do it. But he wouldn't need any pan head screws, that's for sure."

Nick unhooked one hose from the wall. "I need the screws for something I'm doing later."

"No. You don't. You overheard me tell Austin he couldn't have something he wanted, and you thought you'd swoop in and save the day like you do with everyone else."

He shot her an irritated glance. "You have no idea what I do with everyone else." He let the end of the cold water hose fall on the tile floor. Water dripped out and made a small puddle. "We've seen each other at least once a week for the past few months and this is the longest conversation we've ever had."

True. And she couldn't wait for it to end.

"Every time I so much as say hello, you act wicked nervous," he continued. "If I did something to—"

"You didn't."

He grinned. "Good. Because seeing as how we're

probably going to run into each other quite often—and considering that you're working for my sister—why don't we try to at least be friends?"

She narrowed her eyes. Did he really think he could charm her into believing he was the type of guy who did nice things for people out of the goodness of his heart? She didn't care if he was considered around town to be a prince among men. She didn't trust him.

And even if she did, they couldn't be friends. She didn't have any friends.

So what if she got lonely? Or that there were times when she wondered if she could do it all alone. Raise Austin. Keep him safe. Keep their secret. But the decision she'd made when she'd left New York meant she didn't have a choice now.

"We can't be friends," she blurted.

For some reason, that only seemed to amuse him. "Why not?"

"Because I don't like you."

NICK'S SMILE DISAPPEARED. Didn't like him? What the hell? Everyone liked him. Just ask around.

"Maybe if you weren't in such a hurry to get away from me," he claimed irritably, "you'd learn to like me."

"I don't like you getting your hero worship fix from my son."

"Hero worship?" He clenched the wrench he still held, and gave it a backhanded toss into his toolbox. Faith jumped when it hit the handle with a loud clang.

"Funny how we've barely spoken, and yet you have no trouble coming up with a shitty opinion of me."

"You had no right to involve yourself in my personal life—"

"I wasn't trying to stick my nose into your business." He hated losing control, even for a moment. "Austin seemed upset…"

"Sad to say, life is full of disappointments. And while I don't relish the idea, Austin is going to have to deal with not always having things go his way." She dumped the rest of her coffee into the utility sink and rinsed out the cup, her movements jerky.

"I was trying to help."

"I didn't want or need your help. You don't need to befriend the struggling single mother. I'm not one of your sisters."

"What the hell is that supposed to mean?"

"You're at their beck and call."

He scowled down at her. "Lady, you don't know what you're talking about."

"Really? Let's see…" She gestured toward the washing machine. "You're here, on what I'm assuming is your day off…?"

She paused and looked at him expectantly. What else could he do? He nodded once and she continued. "And what are you doing on this gorgeous morning? You're changing water hoses."

"They needed to be replaced and—"

"Yes, they did, but Britney could've done it."

"Britney can't tell a wrench from a screwdriver."

"If you'd teach her how to take care of things herself, she wouldn't have to have someone ride to her rescue all the time." Though Nick had at least five inches on Faith, she somehow managed to look down her nose at him. "I didn't want or need your help with Austin. What I want is for you to keep your nose out of my business."

"So you'd rather have your pride than accept a helping hand every once in a while?"

She flushed, but he couldn't tell if it was from embarrassment or anger. "I don't need your charity."

"You think I don't understand what it's like for Austin, sitting here while you work? How bored he is?" Nick clamped his lips shut. The last thing he wanted was to open up to her about how he knew exactly how the kid felt. Not when she obviously thought so little of him.

His mother might not have dragged him to work with her, but she had left him at home in charge of his sisters. There were plenty of times he'd had to put his needs second.

But he hadn't minded having to quit baseball so he could be home to watch Britney after school, or that he didn't get a video-game system when he was fourteen because they'd needed new snow tires for the car. He had a responsibility to his mother and sisters—the same responsibility Faith Lewis felt for her son. Family did for each other. So why did she think his favors for his sisters were anything different?

"I thought Austin would like something to read to pass the time," he continued. "But if I was out of line, I apologize."

Then, because he didn't care one way or the other if she accepted his apology, he went back to the washer. Kneeling, he unscrewed the hoses from the back of the machine. Water dribbled onto his hands and he wiped them on his jeans. After a moment, he heard the sound of her footsteps as she walked away. Too bad she'd left her soft floral scent behind.

How the hell had she twisted his simple gesture into something to be pissed about? He pinched the bridge of his nose. Even after being surrounded by females his entire life, he still found them a mystery.

"Ms. Garey wants you to come out when you're done," Britney said as she entered the room. "Her niece is visiting next week and she was wondering if you'll take her out."

"I'm busy."

"I didn't even tell you what days she'll be here," Britney said. "Oh, and Ms. Garey wanted me to remind you of how she let you retake some English final your senior year so you could graduate with the rest of your class instead of suffering the humiliation of summer school."

He grabbed the new hoses, viciously tightening the connection for the cold water one. "Blackmail is illegal."

"Hey, you're the cop. You tell her."

Nick tilted his head to the side. Why him? He was a decent guy. What had he done to deserve this? "Is this the same niece she set me up with a few years back? The vegan?" He connected the hot water hose. The wrench slipped and he whacked his knuckle. Pressing his lips together against the pain, he shook his hand. "Because

I'll tell you right now, I'm not eating one bite of her tofu casserole or whatever it was she cooked up for me the last time."

"Take her to the Wave Runner. She can get the all-you-can-eat salad bar."

"And spend the night listening to her lecture me about eating lobster? No thanks." He stood and dropped the dripping hoses into the utility sink. He grimaced when he finally saw his sister. "What the hell are you not quite wearing?"

"Now, Nicky, if I've told you once, I've told you a hundred times, I'm a grown woman and I can dress however I want."

The headache that had started when Faith ripped into him intensified. "True. But I'm pretty sure I can write you up for indecent exposure. Aren't you supposed to wear that vest over something? Like a shirt?"

She adjusted the hem of her top. "For your information, Michael likes the way I dress."

And the last thing he needed to hear was how his baby sister's latest unemployed, stringy-haired, dumber-than-Nick's-firearm boyfriend liked her to show lots of skin. "I'll sleep better tonight knowing that. Toss me a towel, will you?"

Britney handed him one from the dryer, then leaned against the washing machine while he sopped up the water on the floor and put his tools away. "If you had a steady girlfriend, you wouldn't have to go out with the mean old vegan."

He locked his toolbox and stood. "No."

"Why not? Faith is sooo nice and she's smart and funny and—"

"And she's off her rocker. She's also mighty ticked off at me, so even if I was interested—which I'm not— I don't think you'd be able to convince her we're destined to be together."

"What do you mean, she's ticked? What did you do?" Britney asked suspiciously.

He folded the towel and laid it on top of the washing machine. "What makes you think I did anything?"

"Now, don't get all sensitive." Britney poured a cup of coffee, added creamer and handed it to him before getting a bottled water out of the fridge. "Come on. Spill."

He quickly filled her in.

"That doesn't sound like Faith," she said thoughtfully. "Although she is very protective of Austin. Maybe she was just worried about him going that far on his own?"

"Maybe," Nick conceded. But he had a feeling whatever had set Faith off was more than that. His cell phone rang. "Coletti," he said after opening it.

"Nicky," his sister Andrea said, "please tell me you're not busy."

He turned his back on the new hoses. "I'm not busy. What's up?"

"Marie called. Isaac's sick. Marie thinks it's chicken pox." Their sister Marie ran the day care center Andrea's two kids, five-year-old Isaac and two-year-old Dana, attended. "He needs to be picked up, but I can't get away from work until two-thirty and Tuesdays Steve is at his Brunswick office and—"

"And you need me to go get Isaac."

"If you don't have any other plans," she said in a rush. "I'd really appreciate it."

So much for meeting a few buddies for an afternoon golf game. "No problem." He wedged the phone between his shoulder and ear and shoved the washing machine back in place. "Tell Marie I'll be there in ten minutes."

"Thanks, Nicky."

"Isaac's sick," he told Britney after he hung up. "Marie thinks it's the start of chicken pox."

"I told Andrea she'd regret not getting those kids vaccinated."

"Her choice." He picked up his toolbox.

"Wait." Britney grabbed his free wrist. "You can't go until you've made up with Faith."

"Hey, even though I didn't do anything wrong, I already apologized." He'd figured, correctly, it would be the easiest way to get her to lay off.

"Great. Now you two can put this behind you—"

"Are your braids too tight?" The last thing he needed was some high-strung, antagonistic woman in his life.

"Fine." Britney flipped one of those braids over her shoulder. "But you're making a mistake by giving up. You and Faith would be great together. Don't forget, I inherited Great-grandma's sight."

"The only thing you inherited was a tendency to overdramatize situations."

He took it back. She must've also inherited their Nonna's ability to skewer a man with one dark look. "I was going to make you chicken parmigiana for fixing the washing machine," Brit said with an indignant sniff, "but just for that, all you're getting is a thank-you card." She then whirled around on the heel of one of her cowboy boots and sashayed out of the room.

Nick shut his eyes. *God, please save me from the women in my life.*

Amen.

He hoped Britney listened this time. She'd been after him to ask Faith out ever since she'd first hired her. What Brit wasn't aware of was that he'd given in and had invited Faith out to dinner a few months ago. An invitation she'd quickly and politely declined.

He didn't need to be told no twice.

CHAPTER THREE

TEN MINUTES AFTER FAITH got home from work that evening, the phone rang. She remained where she was, staring into the refrigerator, hoping she might find inspiration for dinner. "Austin, can you get that, please?"

The second ring ended abruptly. "It's for you," Austin called from the living room.

Shutting the refrigerator, she grabbed a washed apple out of the bowl on the table and headed into the other room. From his prone position on the sofa, Austin held the phone out, his nose buried in that blasted comic book.

For about the hundredth time that day, she felt guilty over not letting Austin get the comic in the first place. She was so very tired of feeling guilty all the time. But she doubted she'd get any reprieve, seeing as how her list of sins was so damn long.

Like forcing Austin to leave his prized comic book collection behind two towns ago. Which was what happened when you took off in the middle of the night as if the devil himself were after you.

Unfortunately, that's exactly who they were running from. And he would never stop searching for them.

She bit into her apple, then took the phone, holding the mouthpiece against her stomach as she chewed and swallowed. She swatted the tops of Austin's sneakers with the back of her hand. "Get those dirty shoes off my couch."

"Yes, ma'am," he said, not looking up from the comic as he toed his shoes off onto the floor.

Faith pursed her lips and gave him her best Mom stare until he lifted his head. "What?" he asked.

"Put your shoes away," she said around another bite.

"But I just got to the good part."

She nodded toward his shoes. "Go."

He groaned and rolled his eyes.

She lifted the phone to her ear as someone knocked on the door.

"I'll get it," Austin said, rushing past her.

"Check to see who it is first," she reminded him, then said into the phone, "Hello?"

"Hey, it's me," Britney said. "Now, promise you won't get mad…"

Faith watched Austin move aside the curtain covering the door's window. "That is so not a good lead-in."

Whoever knocked must not be a stranger, because Austin undid the dead bolt and opened the door.

"You're right," Britney admitted, "and you can be mad, but remember, I'm doing this because I want to help you."

"I don't suppose that help involves an idea of what to cook for dinner using half a pound of ground beef, two carrots and some stale saltines?"

"Uh…no. Sorry. But this is better," Britney promised. "I got you a surprise."

"I hate surprises." Faith bit into the apple again as Austin stepped aside, giving her a clear view of her doorstep. She inhaled sharply and coughed to dislodge a piece of apple from her windpipe. "Never mind," she choked out. "It's here."

"Already? He was supposed to give me time to prepare you first."

Phone still at her ear, Faith walked over and stood behind Austin, who tipped his head back to look up at her. "Mr. Coletti's here," he said.

"I can see that." She made the mistake of meeting Nick's unflinching, cool gaze. In her stomach, it felt as if a baby bird was about to take flight. "Why don't you put your shoes away and then set the table for me?"

"Are you talking to me?" Britney asked.

"Now why on earth would I ask you to put away your shoes?" Faith said.

"Well, I did leave them by the door…"

Faith smiled and shook her head. "I was talking to Austin. Just…hold on a minute, would you?" She nudged Austin's shoulder.

"Bye," he told Nick.

"See ya, Austin."

She waited until her son was out of earshot. "Britney says you didn't give her time to prepare me." Still holding the phone to her ear, she kept her other hand on the door frame, blocking his entrance to her home. Her sanctuary.

If he didn't get the message she didn't want him here, he wasn't as bright as she'd given him credit for.

He set his toolbox on the blue-painted wooden porch. "Should I come back later?"

"Tell him not to go anywhere," Britney demanded. "Even if you're mad at him—"

"I never said that." She bit into her apple. Hey, she hadn't eaten anything since she'd tried to finish her leftover ham sandwich hours earlier. She was too hungry to worry about crunching in someone's ear.

"He told me how you got upset about him paying Austin to run an errand."

Her face heating, Faith leaned against the doorjamb. As soon as she'd walked away from Nick that morning she'd known she'd been out of line. But her fear that he'd been trying to somehow get close to her son by giving Austin something he wanted so badly had overridden her good sense.

"And now he's standing on my porch with a toolbox at his feet because…why?" Faith asked.

"I asked him to look at your water heater."

"I'd hate to put him out," Faith said, straightening.

Nick hooked his thumbs in his front pockets and rocked back on his heels. She squeezed her apple so hard, she half expected to wind up with sauce on her hands.

"He might be able to fix it, which will save you from having to pay a plumber—a plumber who might not even get to it for days. If Nick can't figure out what's wrong, he'll collect his tools and go home. No harm done."

No harm done? The harm was having Nick Coletti in her house, in her personal business.

"Crap," Britney said. "Michael's beeping for me. I have to go. Just let Nicky look at it, okay?"

She hung up in Faith's ear.

"What's the verdict?" Nick asked, as if he couldn't care less one way or the other what she decided.

"I'm not sure why Britney asked you to come over—"

"She's got a big heart. It's her greatest weakness."

"And you're enabling that weakness?"

"I have a hard time telling her no. Besides, she laid it on thick, told me how much she'd consider it a personal favor to her…."

"She guilted you into coming over here?"

"She's good at convincing people to do what she wants," he said, so solemnly that Faith blinked. "She thought if I helped you with your water heater problem, it'd make up for you being ticked off at me and we could all hold hands, sing songs of friendship and skip off over some fairy-tale rainbow."

Faith cleared her throat. "I don't think that'll ever happen."

"Yeah, well, Brit wants everyone to get along. She's always been that way, even as a kid." He tapped the toolbox with the toe of his work boot. "She loves me and considers you a friend, so she wants us to tolerate each other."

Panic knifed through Faith. Friends? Her and Britney? Why did all the Colettis want to be her friend? Britney was her boss. Period. Besides, when you were friends with people they did things like send their brother to your house. She hadn't missed all those hints Britney had given her these past few months about how wonderful Nick was, how perfect he'd be for some lucky woman.

That lucky woman obviously being Faith.

"If you want me gone," Nick said, "just say the word."

Oh, she wanted. But she'd long since learned that it didn't matter what she wanted.

She'd play nice with Nick, show him she was just a single mother trying to get by, and then he'd stop looking at her as if she was a suspect in one of his cases.

Damn it, she and Austin were done running. And Nick Coletti wasn't going to change that.

"I APPRECIATE YOU checking the water heater." Faith sounded sincere. So why did Nick have the feeling she'd rather eat her apple core then let him in?

"No problem." He picked up his toolbox and stepped over the threshold, his bare arm brushing against hers, causing his skin to prickle with awareness.

Faith shrank back as if she wished she could disappear into the wall. She shut the door. "Uh…it's in the basement."

Nick nodded and took the room in with a quick glance. She sure liked bright colors. If the porch hadn't proved that, her living room did. The walls were painted a sunny yellow, the plump sofa was green with pink-and-white pillows that matched the high-backed, pink-checked chair in the corner. He squinted and hoped all the cheeriness didn't burn his retinas.

Talk about a surprise. Going by how she dressed, he

would've guessed Faith's home to be more subdued. And much more beige.

He followed her as she put the phone back in its receiver on a small green-painted table next to the sofa before going into the long kitchen. The cupboards had been painted white and in the middle of the room stood a narrow island with a cooktop on one side and an eating bar on the other, flanked by two high-backed wooden stools.

Austin sat on one of the stools, reading. "I'll get dinner going as soon as I show Mr. Coletti where the water heater is," Faith told her son.

Nick shifted his toolbox to his other hand. "Why don't you let Austin show me where it is? That way you can go ahead and work on dinner."

She looked at him as if he'd asked her the impossible. See? It was things like that, along with her reaction to his giving Austin that five bucks, that had him so damn curious about her.

"That's not necessary," she assured him, tossing the apple core into the garbage can in the corner. "It'll only take a min—"

"I don't want him to lead me into battle," Nick interrupted. There he was, trying to do her a favor, and she acted as if she didn't trust him around her kid. "If it makes you feel better, why don't you point me in the general direction of the basement? I'm sure with a map, a compass and maybe a decent GPS unit, I'll find my way before nightfall."

"That won't be necessary." But her tone indicated it wasn't altogether out of the realm of possibility, either.

"It's okay, Mom," Austin said. "I'll show him."

He jumped off the stool and Nick followed him to a door at the end of the room. Austin flipped on a light and led the way down the wooden stairs, trailing his hand along the stone walls as he descended. The farther down they went, the cooler it got. And the mustier it smelled.

Nick followed Austin past the washer and dryer, a furnace that had to be at least as old as his mother, and a few large plastic totes that had "Winter Clothes" printed neatly on the sides. That was it for storage.

He set his toolbox down, opened the lid and took out his trouble light. "I take it your mom's not the sentimental type?"

Austin wiped the back of his hand under his nose. "Huh?"

Spotting an outlet, Nick plugged the hanging light in and flipped it on. Laid it on the floor, where light shot up onto Austin's pale face. The kid sure didn't spend much time outside. When Nick was Austin's age, he'd already turned two shades darker. Of course, his olive complexion tanned easily, whereas Austin seemed to take after his fair-skinned mother. That and his eyes were about the only similarities between mother and son.

"Sentimental. You know, mushy about baby clothes and old toys. Most moms keep everything from drawings you made when you were three, to your first lost tooth, to all your report cards."

His mother's basement wasn't half this size, but she'd managed to stuff it with a whole lot more than Faith had. Hell, when Nick had gone down last winter to change her furnace filter, he'd spied his old hockey skates. Why did women hold on to stuff like that?

Austin shrugged. "My mom's not like that. She says the most important thing is that we're together, not holding on to material things."

And if that wasn't a direct quote from Faith, Nick would eat his badge.

"Your mom's right. People are more important than things." Although he couldn't imagine any mother who didn't have at least a small box of keepsakes. But if Faith had one, she didn't keep it in this eerily empty basement. "And now you have more room to store all your winter stuff." When Austin stared at him blankly, Nick added, "Things like your sleds, shovels, boots and hats and gloves. Not to mention all your holiday decorations."

"We don't have any of that," Austin said.

Nick searched for somewhere to hang his light, trying not to reveal what he was thinking. It was weird they didn't have any winter gear. Weird, but hardly illegal, or any reason for his instincts to be kicking in. There could be a reasonable explanation. "I take it you've never lived up north during winter before? Never been around snow?"

Austin shook his head—either as a negative response or to flip his hair out of his eyes. "Nah, I've seen snow. We had a shovel and I even had a sled when we lived in Serenity Springs and—"

Guilt and panic, two emotions Nick saw often when he interrogated suspects, flashed across Austin's face. Apprehension, suspicion, tickled the back of Nick's neck. He rubbed at it but the tickle wouldn't go away.

He wasn't going to interrogate the kid—just ask him a few questions. Maybe get a feel for the real story behind Faith's secretiveness. What was the worst that could happen? If he was wrong, getting the kid to talk about himself wouldn't hurt anything.

Hey, he was a cop. He justified using sneaky tactics all the time.

"What kind of sled did you have?" Nick asked.

"A round, plastic one," Austin muttered, staring at the floor.

"My nephew has one of those," he said, giving up on hanging his light. Hopefully, it'd cast enough of a glow from the floor for him to see what he was doing. "That thing really flies."

"Yeah, it was sweet." The boy scratched at a scab on his knee. "I don't have it anymore. We, uh, decided to move, and I couldn't take it with us."

"You must've had a ton of stuff if you couldn't find room for a sled that size."

"Mom said it would be easier to buy a new one."

"Can't argue with that logic. Better watch out," Nick said. "I'm going to turn the water on to see if I can figure out where the leak came from."

"It came from the bottom."

"You sure? Not from any of the pipes or maybe this faucet?" He squatted and pointed to the brass faucet at the bottom of the tank.

Austin squatted, too, mimicking Nick's stance. "Nah. It sort of poured out of the bottom."

"Let's double-check."

He stood, reached up and twisted a handle. No sooner had he moved back than water streamed out from the bottom of the tank.

"Damn." Nick stepped over the water to shut off the valve again.

"Told you," Austin gloated. "Sir," he added quickly, when Nick glanced over his shoulder at him. But Nick noticed he was fighting a grin.

Which was good. The times he'd been around Austin, the kid had seemed too serious. Too mature.

Neither of which any nine-year-old boy worth his salt should be.

Having already figured out the water heater was toast, Nick stepped over the small puddle of water. "Got any towels handy so I can clean up this mess?"

"Sure." Austin ran off, coming back almost immediately with a large bath towel.

"Thanks." Nick knelt and mopped up the water. "Do you play baseball? We have a short rec league that starts soon. Sign-ups are this weekend if you're interested."

Longing filled Austin's eyes. "I don't play baseball."

"No? What about midget football? Or if you're into skating, we have a youth hockey league—"

"No!" Austin's hands were now fisted at his sides, his shoulders rigid, his lips a thin line. "I mean…no, thank you. I…I don't want to play any sports."

"Hey, it's no problem."

Austin nodded and blew out a breath. Either he had a personal—and vehement—hatred of organized sports or there was a whole lot more going on with this kid than Nick had realized.

"So, you've lived in a lot of difference places?" Nick asked. Austin shrugged, which Nick took to mean yes. "How are you liking it here?"

"It's okay."

"Where did you live before you moved to Kingsville?"

When he got no response, Nick glanced up. Austin shrugged again. "Just around."

Nick tightened his grip on the towel. Obviously Austin took after his mother in more ways than just his eye color. Trying to get to know him was like trying to convince Britney to stop dressing like a sixteen-year-old pop star. Both were exercises in futility.

And frustrating as hell.

"Around, huh? What about that town you mentioned earlier? Serenity Springs? How long did you—"

"I have to go," Austin said, his face red, his eyes suspiciously shiny.

Nick straightened, the wet towel in his hand dripping onto his shoe as he watched Austin race up the stairs. You'd have thought he'd suggested the kid go play in traffic or something.

He walked to the washing machine and dropped the towel into an empty laundry basket. There was something going on with Faith and Austin. The kid had looked so guilty when he'd mentioned Serenity Springs, it was as if he'd just blurted out a state secret.

Nick already knew they'd moved around a lot before settling in Kingsville. Britney had gleaned that much information from her employee. But not much else. Nick hadn't really wondered about it before. He'd figured they hadn't found the right place to settle.

But now…now he couldn't ignore the little voice in the back of his head. The one telling him there was more to the story. The one whispering that maybe Faith and Austin were running from something.

Or someone.

CHAPTER FOUR

STEPPING ONTO THE first stair, Faith stopped short when Austin came barreling around the corner. "Hey," she said as he took the stairs two at a time, "I was just coming down to see how things were going."

Because though she'd been telling herself he was fine, she couldn't stop worrying. He'd rarely been alone with any other adult since they'd left New York, and she'd made sure he was never alone with a man. Nick was the golden boy of Kingsville. Well liked. Honorable. A man people turned to when they needed help. But she knew all too well that a spotless reputation was no guarantee of a man's true nature.

"It's going fine," Austin mumbled, brushing past her.

She caught up with him by the sink. "Are you sure?" She searched his face. His cheeks were pink and he kept his gaze averted. Her fingers tensed on his shoulders. "Did something happen? Did—did Nick say...or do...something to you?"

Austin pulled away from her. "No."

"If someone upsets you or makes you feel...uncomfortable...you need to tell me."

"Nothing happened."

She straightened at the tone in his voice. "I'm glad to hear that. But how about you lose the attitude? Or at least save some up until you hit your teens."

"Sorry," he said, as the sound of footsteps climbing the stairs reached them.

"I have some bad news." Nick set his toolbox down by her most prized flea-market find, an antique pedestal table with a distressed white finish. "I also have some almost good news."

"Can I finish reading my comic now?" Austin asked.

"Sure," Faith said slowly. "But only for fifteen minutes. Then I'm going to need you to set the table and take the garbage out."

"Yes, ma'am."

"Bye, Austin," Nick called as the boy walked away. Her son lifted a hand but kept right on going.

"I'll take the bad news first," she told Nick, vowing to talk to Austin about his lack of manners once they were alone. If he said nothing had happened in the basement, she had no reason to doubt him, but she couldn't shake the feeling there was more going on than her son had told her.

"You need a new water heater," Nick announced.

"I figured as much." She washed her hands and began mixing the ingredients together for meat loaf. Cold, raw beef squished between her fingers. "I appreciate you taking time out of your day off to look at it."

He stood at the counter next to her. "Don't you want to hear the almost good news?"

What she wanted was to show him the door. Too bad she had a part to play. "Of course."

"I called a friend of mine. He can get you a new water heater at cost. Plus, if I help him install it, he'll give you a break on the labor."

"Why would he do that?"

"Because I asked him to."

She was becoming even more jaded than she'd realized if the idea of someone doing a friend a favor made her suspicious.

She shaped the meat mixture into a small loaf, set it in a glass baking dish and washed her hands. "I wouldn't feel right imposing on him, or you, that way."

It was funny how things worked out. She'd spent most of her life searching for a man to take care of her, and now when a guy did offer his help, she couldn't get away fast enough. Yeah, life sure was a freaking riot.

"It's no imposition on either of us," Nick assured her. "He'll still get paid, but it's up to you. It won't save you a lot, just a couple hundred dollars."

"Did he happen to mention how much he thinks it'll cost?"

Nick named a figure that, while still high enough to make her checkbook whimper, was two hundred dollars less than the quote the plumber had given her over the phone this morning. She stuck the meat loaf into the preheated oven, rinsed two small potatoes and picked up her coarse vegetable brush.

It was only one more time, a few more hours of having Nick in here, around her son. And he wouldn't really even have to be around them. She could leave Nick and his friend to do their job while she and Austin steered clear. Surely they could get through it unscathed.

"On second thought," she said, scrubbing the potato so hard she almost took the skin right off, "I'd be… grateful for your help."

"No problem. We'll swing by tomorrow after work. It shouldn't take more than an hour or so to finish the job. Six o'clock work for you?"

"Sounds good." Could he stop staring at her now? She'd given in. What more did he want? Pleasant conversation? That was just way beyond her acting capabilities at the moment. Besides, she needed to get back to Austin, to reassure herself he really was okay.

She set the potatoes aside and, inwardly cringing at her own rudeness, said, "I guess I'll see you tomorrow, then."

As a nudge, it was less than subtle, but at least it worked. Humor lit his dark eyes. "Right. I can find my own way out."

"Oh, no, let me just—"

But he picked up his toolbox and left, with Faith racing after him. She stopped in the doorway to find Nick crouching next to the couch, talking to Austin.

"I was apologizing," Nick said to her, even though he didn't look her way, just watched her son while Austin kept his gaze glued to his comic book.

Her stomach dropped. "Apologizing for what?"

"I'm not exactly sure." Nick drummed his fingers against his knee. "But I think it had something to do with my asking if Austin was interested in playing baseball."

"I'm not," he muttered.

"Yeah." Nick nodded. "I got that. Anyway," he told Austin, "I didn't want you to think I was trying to pressure you—"

"I didn't," the boy said, still not so much as glancing Nick's way.

"Does that mean we're okay?"

Austin lifted a shoulder. Faith opened her mouth to scold him but caught the quick head shake Nick gave her. "Great." Nick stood and grabbed his toolbox once again. "I guess I'll see you tomorrow."

He held out his fist. For a moment, Faith had no idea what he was doing until Austin, still staring at the comic, bumped his own fist against the man's much larger one. Nick grinned, gave her a wink and walked out the door.

Faith watched him leave.

Then she crossed the room and locked the door behind him.

"HOW COME I GOT this end?" Nick asked the next evening, struggling down Faith's steps backward while he and Ethan Crosby hauled a new water heater to the basement.

"Quit bitching. I had the low end when we moved that Ping-Pong table, remember? And that thing weighs at least fifty pounds more than this." Ethan shifted his side of the heater a few inches higher. "I have two kids to send to college—"

"They're both still in diapers."

"—and I can't risk having my neck broken because you can't hold up your end."

"Get over it," Nick said, referring to Christmas Eve two years ago when Ethan had helped him move an assembled Ping-Pong table into Kathleen's basement. "You only needed four stitches."

Nick took a careful step backward, his arms stretched wide to hold on to the bulky, heavy box. He glanced over his shoulder.

Three more steps and they made it to the bottom without any casualties. Most importantly, they made it without dropping the damn thing. After carrying it to the far end of the basement, they set it upright and took a moment to catch their breath.

Faith came down carrying a tray with a pitcher of lemonade, two glasses and a small plate of chocolate chip cookies. She faltered when she spotted them, but it was so brief, Nick doubted Ethan even noticed.

"I'll just leave this here," she said, setting the tray down on top of the short stack of storage totes. She wore baggy jeans and an oversize black T-shirt. He wondered if she even owned a pair of shorts. And what her figure looked like under all those shapeless clothes she insisted on wearing. "Uh…if you need anything, I'll be outside."

Ethan smiled. "Thanks."

She returned his smile with a nervous one of her own and went back upstairs, her thick ponytail swinging in time with her movements. Ethan picked up a cookie and took a bite.

"How about you eat when we're done?" Nick asked, grabbing a plastic bucket. "I'd like to get home in time to watch the ball game."

"Game doesn't start for two hours." Ethan helped himself to another cookie, then wiped his hand on the side of his khaki work pants. "And you're not usually in a hurry to get away from a pretty woman. Usually they can't wait to get away from you."

Nick set the bucket underneath the spigot and turned it on to drain the remaining water from the heater. "The only reason I'm doing this is because Brit nagged me into it."

"Bullshit," Ethan said cheerfully. "You're interested in Ms. Lewis. What's the matter? She have enough sense not to be interested back?"

"I wonder," Nick said thoughtfully, tapping a wrench against his palm, "what Lauren would say if she discovered what really happened the night of your bachelor party."

Ethan's smirk faded. "That's cold, man. She can't ever find out about that."

Nick feigned a puzzled expression. "No? Huh."

"I was drunk."

"I'll tell you what. I'll keep my mouth shut about her dog's Mohawk—and who really held the clippers—and you can keep your mouth shut about me and Faith Lewis."

Eating another cookie, Ethan shrugged belligerently, which Nick took as a yes. Nick slapped his friend's shoulder. "It's a sad state of affairs when a man is afraid of his one-hundred-and-ten-pound wife."

Ethan snorted. "About as sad as a man putting in a new water heater for a woman who's clearly not interested."

Damn. No wonder his mother always warned him not to gloat.

Once the water stopped draining, Nick took the bucket upstairs. Opening the kitchen door that led out into Faith's tiny backyard, he was met by the loud rumble of a lawn mower shaking the hell out of Austin as he cut the grass. Squinting against the sunlight, Nick crossed over to the side of Faith's one-stall garage, where she knelt weeding a flower bed.

Like the inside of her house, the small garden was a riot of colors. White, yellows, pinks and blues filled the base, but the centerpiece was a bright purple clematis winding its way up the sides and around the rungs of an old wooden ladder leaning against the wall.

She stood and met him by the edge of the garage. "Everything going all right?" she asked over the sound of the mower.

"Fine." He set the bucket at her feet. "We had to drain the heater and I thought you could use this to water your flowers."

She wore dark sunglasses, so he couldn't see her expression. "That's very…environmentally sound of you."

"I'm all about reducing, reusing and recycling," he said soberly.

"Really?" She took off her dirt-encrusted garden gloves, held them in one hand while trying to untangle hair caught in her sunglasses with the other. "I never would've guessed you were so green-minded."

"Here," he said, edging closer, "let me help."

She stiffened as he gently extricated her hair from the small hinge and tucked the silky strands behind her ear. He let his hand drop and curled his fingers into his palm.

"I would try and tell you that Al Gore has always been a personal hero of mine," he continued, trying to put her back at ease—if she ever was at ease with him, "but the truth is, I promised my nephew Isaac I'd do my best to save the planet."

Acting as if it took her entire concentration, she stepped back and brushed the dirt from the knees of her jeans. "Sounds like a pretty big job for one man."

"Isaac's five. He pretty much thinks that since I'm a police officer, I'm something of a superhero."

And why that made her wince, he had no idea.

"Every little bit helps. And since we're not due to get rain for a few days, this—" she tapped the bucket with the toe of her worn sneakers "—will come in handy. Thank you."

"That kills you, doesn't it?"

She swallowed. "Wha…what does?"

"The few times you've thanked me, it's as if someone's dragging the words out of your mouth."

"Don't be silly. I appreciate you helping me like this." She raised her head, and though he couldn't see past her dark lenses, he sensed she was looking him dead in the eye. "Truly."

He also sensed she was lying through her teeth.

"I'd better get back," he said, not wanting to push her too far. He nodded toward a very sweaty, red-faced Austin. "It'll take a while for the water to warm up in the tank, but I don't think Austin will mind rinsing off under the hose today."

"He'll love it. Why little boys can stand under the

freezing spray from a hose for hours, but hate the confines of a tub or shower, I'll never know."

Nick grinned. "The hose is more of an adventure. And if there's one thing males of all ages can't get enough of, it's an adventure."

Another thing they couldn't get enough of was a challenge. At least Nick couldn't resist one. And at the moment, his biggest challenge was figuring out the woman in front of him.

"We should be finished and out of your hair in no time," he said before walking back into the house.

No, he wasn't interested in Faith, at least not the way Ethan accused him of. But Nick was curious. Back inside the house, he watched Faith through the kitchen window. She crouched and began yanking weeds, tossing them into a small pile. He couldn't quite figure her out, but he aimed to try.

She obviously loved bright colors, so why did she dress in such muted tones? Add that to her jumpiness around him, her obviously not wanting him alone with Austin, and the kid's rush to get away from him yesterday and Nick couldn't help but think he'd seen this situation many times before.

He'd been called to his fair share of domestic disputes, and each one of them had made his stomach turn. He'd also seen the results of that abuse. How the victims blamed themselves for the violence. And believed they could never get away from their abuser. Was that what made Faith and Austin so secretive? Had some bastard laid his hand on them?

Though Faith showed signs indicating she might have been abused, Nick wasn't going to jump to conclusions. He needed more evidence to prove his instincts were right. He wanted to help them. And there was only one way he'd be able to do that.

He needed to earn their trust.

LESS THAN AN HOUR LATER, Nick and Ethan had her new water heater installed and the old one in the back of Ethan's pickup. Standing in her freshly mowed backyard, Faith handed Ethan an envelope with the money she owed him.

"I really can't thank you enough for coming today," she said, her voice steady and almost pleasant. She even added a smile. After Nick's remark about how strained she sounded whenever she thanked someone, she realized she needed to shore up her acting skills.

"Glad I could help out," Ethan said. He was a big man, as fair as Nick was dark, with white-blond hair and pale blue eyes. He seemed harmless.

Nick, on the other hand, was a whole other story.

Last night as she'd tucked Austin into bed, he'd admitted he'd inadvertently told Nick they'd once lived in Serenity Springs. That, combined with her nervousness around Nick getting the better of her, convinced her she needed to be friendlier. More open and honest. To show Nick she had nothing to hide.

Even if it was all a lie.

"I was…" She cleared her throat. "I was hoping you would allow me to treat you both to dinner."

"Excuse me?" Nick asked.

"Now I don't have to go the rest of the week without hot water, not to mention the money I was able to save. I just wanted to thank you. Both."

Nick searched her face. "Let me get this straight. You're volunteering to spend more time with me?"

She ground her back teeth together. He just couldn't make this easy, could he? "Yes. I thought the four of us could go to Nero's for pizza."

Ethan glanced from one to the other. "I'm afraid Nick's in a hurry to get home. Something about a baseball game."

"That game's not on until tomorrow," he countered.

Ethan's pale eyebrows shot up. "It's not?"

"Nope. I'd love to have pizza with you and Austin."

"I must've heard wrong then," Ethan said. "And I'd be happy to join—"

"But he can't," Nick interjected smoothly.

"I can't?"

"He needs to get home to watch his kids," Nick explained. "Tonight's Lauren's yoga class at the Y."

"It's Wednesday," Ethan pointed out. "Yoga is on Tue—"

"Mohawk."

Faith frowned. "What's going on?"

"Nothing." Nick seemed as innocent as a newborn. She didn't buy it for a moment. "I just don't want him to be late." He lowered his voice as if Ethan wasn't right there to hear him. "His wife holds grudges when she's mad. One time she made him sleep on the couch for… How long was it?" he asked his friend. "A week?"

"Ten days," Ethan grumbled.

"I'd hate for that to happen again," Nick said, giving his friend a significant look.

"Me, too. Which is why," Ethan said to Faith, "I can't accept your dinner invitation."

"Oh." *Crap*. There went her third-party buffer. "Maybe another time," she said lamely.

"Sure thing. Talk to you later, Nick."

Faith watched Ethan climb into his truck and drive away. Damn. What was she going to do now?

Shoving her sunglasses on top of her head, she faced him. "Since Ethan had to leave, why don't we…postpone that dinner? I'm sure you're anxious to get home."

"Not particularly."

"Still," she said, not caring if she sounded desperate, "it's getting late—"

"It's only seven-twenty."

"But we both have to work tomorrow," she stated.

"Faith, are you trying to renege on your dinner invitation?"

"Of course not," she sputtered. "That would be rude."

"And you're never rude, are you?"

That's right. She'd been a tramp, a liar and a horrible mother who made her precious baby feel guilty if he so much as breathed a word of truth to anyone. She'd broken the law, didn't trust a living soul and was afraid in her zeal to keep Austin safe, she was somehow doing more harm than good. But at least she was always polite.

Nick looked past her and said, "If you and Austin don't want to go to Nero's—"

"We're going to Nero's?" Austin asked as he burst

out of the house, the back door slamming behind him. "When? Now?"

Faith sighed and smoothed her son's wet hair back from his forehead. As Nick had predicted, he'd been more than happy to strip down to his shorts and rinse off outside with the hose. He'd even talked her into letting him wash his hair, shrieking and laughing the entire time he'd doused it with the cold spray.

"I hope you didn't leave your wet clothes and towel on the floor," she said.

"I hung them over the shower rod." He shook her arm. "Are we really going to Nero's?"

"Yeah. We really are."

Austin gave a whoop and she winced.

"Well, now that we have the attention of everyone in town, and out at the marina, we'd better get going." The sooner they left, the sooner they could get back. "Why don't we meet you there?" she asked Nick. Once she sent him on his way, she might be able to fake car trouble. Or a sudden, violent illness. Sure, Austin would be disappointed but—

"It's a nice night," Nick said. "You two up for a walk?"

Her son's eyes widened. "Can we, Mom? Or I could ride my bike?"

And there was no way she could say no. Besides, maybe having dinner with Nick wouldn't be so bad. She'd just have to make certain she worked it to her advantage.

"Sure. I need to get my purse," she called after Austin as he took off toward the garage. "Wait for us out front and stay off the road until I get there."

With him out of sight, she grabbed Nick's wrist and dragged him inside the house.

"Is there a problem?" he asked when they were by the sink.

"That depends." His skin was warm under her fingers. She snatched her hand away. "Did you do that on purpose?"

"Do what on purpose?"

"Did you want him to overhear us? Did you think I'd give in simply because my son wanted pizza?"

"To take your questions in order—yes. And I'd hoped."

Her jaw dropped. "Why would you do something like that? Didn't we already discuss you not interfering with my business?"

"But this wasn't just your business, it was mine, too. You were trying to get out of going to dinner—"

"I wasn't trying to get out of anything," she insisted, her cheeks burning. "I just thought you'd prefer to go another night."

"—but once a pretty woman offers to feed a single guy, he'd be crazy to let that opportunity pass. You see, men have certain basic…needs. So the reason I made it as difficult as possible for you to back out of dinner is pretty simple."

He leaned forward. Her heart sped as she pressed back until the edge of the counter dug into her spine. But even though he was close, he didn't touch her. He just whispered, "I'm hungry."

CHAPTER FIVE

SOMETIMES YOU JUST HAD TO make the most of a lousy situation.

And that's exactly what she'd do, Faith resolved as she and Nick walked down her quiet street toward town. After all, it was a lovely summer evening, warm with a light breeze that brought in the salty scent of the ocean. They'd gone two blocks and so far Nick had kept the conversation off personal subjects. Instead they'd discussed the weather and the new specialty candy shop going in over on Foster Drive.

Boring, yes. But at least he wasn't interrogating her.

Austin zipped past them, legs pumping furiously on the pedals of the bike she'd picked up for him at a garage sale a few weeks ago. He rode ahead, stopped to look for traffic, then made a U-turn and rode back to them—a process he'd repeated numerous times since they'd left the house. His face was flushed, his helmet low on his forehead and his knuckles white where he gripped the handlebars. Best of all, he was smiling. And that was something she never tired of seeing.

It was also something that didn't happen very often

lately. And while she'd like to blame it on his age and hormones, she couldn't. It was her fault. For forcing him to lie, to keep their secrets. But she didn't know what else to do. How else to live.

A car horn sounded and both she and Nick waved at one of her customers. Faith tugged at the hem of her wrinkled shirt. Shoot. She should've changed. Or at least brushed her hair. As a hairdresser, she was a walking billboard for her craft.

Too bad at the moment she was a disheveled mess.

But she'd been so flustered after Nick's comment about being hungry, at his nearness, she couldn't get out of her house fast enough.

She glanced surreptitiously at him. A lock of dark hair fell across his forehead, softening the sharp lines of his profile. She wished he looked more like a police officer tonight and less…normal. Albeit normal in an above average sense. But she had to remember he *was* a cop.

They came to her favorite house on the street, a gorgeous blue Victorian with white accents, dark gray trim, multiple rooflines and a large horseshoe-shaped window in the front. A man with wiry salt-and-pepper hair badly in need of a new style sat in a white wicker rocking chair on the front porch, reading a paperback.

"Evening, Mr. Close," Nick called, causing the man to look up from his book. "Nice weather we're having."

Mr. Close abruptly stopped rocking. Scowling, he got to his feet and muttered something under his breath. He then went inside, slamming the door shut behind him.

Faith's jaw dropped. "Did he call you a *bloody wanker?*"

"Ayup," Nick said, sounding like an old-time Mainer. "Mr. Close is originally from England. He's, uh… holding a bit of a grudge against me."

Though interested—way more than she should be—she wouldn't ask. She didn't want Nick to get the idea that she was curious about him. Yes, her role required her to be friendly, but only to a point. It wasn't as if she was up for an Academy Award.

"Mom! Watch," Austin cried as he came up behind them. "I can do a wheelie." He pedaled past. His front tire barely left the ground before it fell back to earth again, but her heart lodged itself in her throat. He braked. "Did you see?"

"Yes, I saw," she said, injecting what she hoped was the proper amount of enthusiasm. Wasn't nine too young to be trying daredevil tricks? "That's great."

"Looking good, bud," Nick said. "Try pulling back when you lift the handlebars. But be ready to put your feet down if you lose your balance."

"Okay." And he was off to try again.

"Thank you," Faith said drily. "Maybe next you could teach him how to build a ramp so he can practice jumping over tractor trailers."

"Nah. He'd need a motorcycle for that. Although if he got enough speed up, he might make it over a small car."

"That's like music to a mother's ears." She knew better, but she couldn't contain her curiosity any longer.

"Is that what you did to Mr. Close? Taught his son how to jump vehicles?"

"Mr. Close doesn't have a son. Just a daughter. Delia."

"Judging from the reverence in your voice and the smile on your face, I'm guessing Delia was quite pretty?"

"Gorgeous. Plus she had this sexy accent..." He shrugged. "What can I say? I'm a sucker for a lady with an accent."

Thank God Faith had lost her own Southern accent years ago. "Delia's dad had a problem with your interest in her?"

"Not just me. All the guys in school were after her, but her dad was so strict she couldn't date until she was eighteen." Nick shot Faith a grin. "I didn't want to wait. So my sisters told me about some scene in a movie they loved where a guy serenades a girl with his boom box outside her bedroom window."

They stopped at the curb, checked for traffic, then crossed onto Main Street. "No more practice wheelies," Faith told Austin.

"Can I wait for you at the restaurant?" he asked.

She spotted Nero's bright red-and-white awning at the end of the block. "Sure."

Nick took ahold of her arm and tugged her close. She stiffened and would've have pulled away, but before she could, he said, "Just trying to save you from getting entangled in their love." He nodded at the young couple walking toward them.

They were in their late teens, the girl in a tank top and frayed cutoffs, her arm around her boyfriend's slim waist. He was shirtless and wearing low-slung cargo shorts. His scraggly beard was more peach fuzz than actual facial hair, and his hand was in the girl's back pocket. Their heads were bent close together and they only had eyes for each other.

"Oh," Faith mumbled, her face on fire. "Thanks."

Nick let go of her, his fingers sliding slowly against her arm. "No problem."

Ignoring the tingle on her skin, she kept her eyes straight ahead and cleared her throat. *"Say Anything."*

"What's that?"

"The movie your sisters told you about was *Say Anything.*"

She'd loved that movie so much she'd stolen the video from the local rental place when she was fourteen. How she'd wanted nothing more than to have some guy drive up to her cramped trailer and take her away from her miserable life. To care for her.

"Yeah, that sounds right. Anyway, Kathleen and Andrea swore if I recreated that scene, Delia wouldn't be able to resist me. Boy, were they wrong."

He greeted the members of a young family as they passed, before continuing. "I went to her house late one Friday night, pulled out my brand-new portable CD player and blasted Guns N' Roses's 'November Rain.'"

"How romantic."

"What can I say? I was a GN'R fan. It might've gone over better if it hadn't been a mild night in May. But I definitely got Delia's attention. She opened her bedroom window, leaned out and—"

"You two reenacted the balcony scene from *Romeo and Juliet?*" Faith asked, still enough of a romantic to picture it clearly.

"I wish. She told me to get lost. At least, that's what she later claimed she'd been saying. I couldn't hear her over the song. By the time Slash's guitar solo started, Mr. Close had called the police. I could've been booked with disturbing the peace, trespassing and causing a public nuisance. Luckily, I got off with a warning."

Faith searched out Austin, saw him locking his bike to a light pole in front of the restaurant. "Mr. Close never forgave you for waking him up? Or maybe it was your song choice he couldn't overlook."

"I think it had more to do with them discovering Delia wasn't alone in her bedroom." He lowered his voice conspiratorially. "Rumor has it that when they heard the music, Delia's parents rushed into her room to see what was going on. Mrs. Close spied a pair of boxer shorts by Delia's bed and it didn't take them long to find Bobby Shields hiding in the closet. Poor guy didn't even have a chance to pull his jeans on before Mr. Close threw him out into the yard."

"This was the same Delia who wasn't allowed to date?" Faith asked.

"Didn't stop her and Bobby from seeing each other on the sly. Mr. Close still blames me for his discovery that his sweet baby girl was growing up—and defying him right under his nose."

Austin was still messing with his bike lock when she

and Nick reached the pizzeria, so Faith moved aside to let people pass. "But…but what about your happy ending?"

He looked at her curiously. "My what?"

"Your happy ending. The one where you get the girl and drive off into the night. Even *Say Anything* ended with Lloyd and Diane together. All you got was cops showing up and Mr. Close calling you names for the next fifteen years."

It didn't seem fair. But then again, since when was life fair? Hers certainly hadn't been.

"It wasn't how I'd hoped the night would end," Nick admitted, "and I was crushed when I found out about Delia and Bobby—until I went to school Monday. Word of my romantic streak got around and the next thing I knew, girls who'd never looked at me twice were giving me their numbers."

"And Delia and Bobby?"

"They got married right after high school and now run an outdoor store down in Portland. Last I heard, Delia just had a daughter. Their fifth." Nick winked at Faith. "So you see? There was a happy ending, after all."

NICK HELD THE DOOR OPEN for Austin and Faith, not surprised to see how packed it was inside. Nero's had the best pizza in town and even during the slow months did a brisk business.

"There's an empty booth," Austin said, pointing to one next to the large picture window at the front of the building.

"That's fine," Faith said.

She barely got the words out before Austin took off

as if the restaurant would run out of cheese and pepperoni if they didn't snatch that table immediately.

Nick followed Faith through the noisy dining room. Bob Seger's "Night Moves" played on the corner jukebox, competing with conversations and the bells and whistles from the old-style video games next to the hallway that led to the restrooms. Nick glanced over and couldn't miss the longing in Austin's expression as he sat on the edge of the seat staring at the games.

A toddler in one of those one-piece short sets, her pale hair sprouting like a fountain out of a band on top of her head, darted in front of them, causing Faith to stop suddenly.

"Sorry," the little girl's father said, scrambling over to his daughter. He scooped the child up and carried her back to their table. The imp grinned and opened her chubby fist at Nick. He waved back.

Faith stepped forward but Nick caught her around the waist. As with the other times he'd casually touched her, she tensed. He didn't release her, though. Not when he detected some very nice curves underneath her baggy clothes.

He bent his head, his breath ruffling the loose strands of hair over her ear. "Would it be all right if I gave Austin a couple of bucks for the video games?"

Nick's fingers tightened on her waist when she looked at him over her shoulder. "You're asking my permission this time?" she asked.

He dropped his hands. "I'm a quick learner. And I don't often make the same mistake twice."

"That's very nice of you to offer, but I've already set aside a few dollars for him to play the games." Then she walked away.

Nick tried to follow, but was waylaid by Clarise Farrell. By the time he got free, Faith sat in the booth, a glass of iced tea in front of her, while Austin was at the Pac Man machine.

Nick slid into the seat across from her. "Sorry about that."

"Is everything okay?"

"Fine. Mrs. Farrell wanted to tell me that this morning she spotted Donald Kearns walking around in nothing but his underwear again."

"He was roaming the streets in his underwear and she didn't tell the police until now?"

Nick picked up a plastic menu and scanned it. "Mr. Kearns wasn't roaming the streets. He was in his own house, although why he feels the need to hang out in his dining room in his skivvies is beyond me." He noticed Faith's confusion. "They're neighbors. And this isn't the first time Mrs. Farrell has complained. Which is how I know the only way she could see into Mr. Kearns's dining room is if she's in her guest bedroom and stands on a step stool."

"Mr. Kearns must be something to see."

"He's seventy-seven with a potbelly and knobby knees. And I hope like hell that when I stop by his house tomorrow to talk to him—once again—about installing blinds in his dining room windows, he'll get dressed before he answers the door. Unlike last time."

"And some people think small towns are boring."

Their waiter, a teenager with short, spiky dyed-black hair, snakebite piercings on his upper lip and earlobe-stretching studs in his ears, asked, "Can I get you something to drink, sir?"

"I'll have a soda." When the kid left, Nick sat back and laid his arm on the back of the booth. "What do you like on your pizza?"

"Austin and I usually get half plain cheese, half veggie loaded."

"The veggie half must be for Austin."

"He loves nothing more," she deadpanned.

"No pepperoni?" Nick asked, unable to hide his disappointment. Pizza without pepperoni was like sex without kissing. Good, yeah, but somehow lacking. "What about protein?"

"I'm not sure processed meat counts as real protein," she said as their waiter set a can of soda and a plastic glass filled with ice cubes in front of Nick. "But if you want it," Faith hastily added, those impeccable manners of hers kicking in, "please get it. I can always pick it off."

"You can get pepperoni on just a few slices," their waiter assured them, taking a small order form out of his dirty apron pocket. "It's no problem."

"Let's do that then," she said. They placed their order and the kid left. She picked up her straw wrapper, smoothed it out and then rolled it into a short tube. "It's busy," she said. "Here. Tonight, I mean."

"Best pizza on the coast. It'll be even crazier next week."

"Why's that?"

"People will start flocking to town early for the Fourth of July Festival." Nick poured his soda into the glass and took a drink. "Most downtown businesses see an increase of at least ten percent during the summer. Specialty shops and restaurants see a fifteen to twenty percent increase and that can get even higher during the festival weekend."

"We've had a few more walk-ins since summer started," Faith agreed.

"Brit said you suggested she have a sidewalk sale of products and offer specials throughout the month to draw in some tourists."

"It was just an idea."

"She also said you've been helping her a lot… Have you been a hairdresser for long?"

"Since I was eighteen."

"You obviously have some good ideas about running a business," he said. "Do you want your own shop someday?"

Faith tossed the paper aside. "I'm not sure," she said, a tiny frown marring her forehead. "I've never thought about it before."

"So you've never owned a salon? Not even in Serenity Springs?" he asked, watching her carefully.

Her head snapped up. "Where?"

"Serenity Springs." No, he wasn't interrogating her. He was merely curious about her past. Making idle predinner conversation. "Austin mentioned you'd lived there."

She sat back. "Oh." She laughed, but it sounded

forced. "He's always getting the name mixed up. We lived in Serenity Hills, Kentucky. My husband—my ex-husband—worked for a horse-breeding farm down there. That's the last place we lived before the divorce. My ex, he…had a difficult time keeping a job, and all the moving got to be too hard on Austin."

"That why you split up?"

Surprisingly, she didn't take offense to his prying question. "Part of it. It's the same old story. We were high school sweethearts—"

"In Pennsylvania?"

"Excuse me?"

"When Brit first hired you she mentioned you were originally from Pennsylvania."

"Yes, a small town outside of Harrisburg."

"You ever get back there?"

She sipped her tea. "There's no reason. My father took off before I was born and my mother and I had a…falling-out about my decision to get married." Faith's lips thinned. "She was right, but I was too stubborn to admit I'd made a mistake, so I stuck it out. And then I got pregnant. Having a child…changes you." Faith met Nick's eyes. "At least it changed me."

He waited for her to go on. Getting Faith to open up was a lesson in patience. When she didn't continue, he asked, "How did it change you?"

At first he didn't think she'd answer. But then she set her elbows on the table and ran a finger down the condensation on her glass.

"It made me less selfish," she said, so simply he felt as if for the first time she'd been honest with him. "My pride didn't stand a chance against my love for him. I wanted more for Austin than I wanted for myself. I wanted somewhere safe he could call home."

"Think you've found that in Kingsville?"

"I hope so."

He jiggled his glass, shifting the ice in it. "You never reconciled with your mother?"

"By the time I was ready to extend an olive branch, she'd passed on."

"I'm sorry."

Faith lifted a shoulder. Nick drummed his fingers against his cup. For his job, he had to be able to judge people. To read them. So why couldn't he get a handle on Faith? While she hadn't lost the nervous edge she always seemed to have around him, she did seem to at least be trying to relax. And yet he still sensed something was off. That what she'd just told him about her mom was somehow…rehearsed.

"I got to the fifth level," Austin cried as he raced over to their booth.

Faith scooted over so he could sit. "Congratulations."

"That's great," Nick added. "You keep working at it and you'll replace my name on the list of high scorers."

"You play it, too?" Austin asked, as if Nick had said he wore Superman underwear.

"Not since I was a kid."

"Wow," he breathed. "I didn't know Pac Man was *that* old."

"I used to ride my pet brontosaurus here after a hard day of inventing fire," Nick said.

Austin smirked. "There were no humans when dinosaurs lived."

"My mistake. It was my pet woolly mammoth."

Austin laughed and reached for his drink.

"Freeze," Faith said. "Hands."

As she dug into her suitcase-size purse, her son rolled his eyes. Faith squirted some antibacterial gel onto his palms, flipped it closed and dropped it back into her bag.

"I'd be even better at Pac Man," Austin said, giving his mom a sly look, "if I practiced more at home."

"I'm not giving you more game time," Faith said. "Two hours a day is more than enough in front of the TV."

"But I'm not watching TV," he argued. "And video games help develop hand-eye coordination."

"So do lots of other activities," Faith said as their waiter delivered their pizza, along with plates, knives and forks.

Austin set a cheese slice on his plate. "Like what?"

"Like…" She took several napkins out of the dispenser and handed them to him. "Um…"

"Playing catch," Nick interjected.

"I don't have anyone to play catch with," Austin mumbled, cutting off the tip of his pizza with the side of his fork and popping it into his mouth.

Faith chose her own piece, a veggie one farthest from the slices with the pepperoni. "We played catch last week."

"She throws like a girl," he told Nick in a loud whisper.

"I can see where that would be a problem," Nick murmured.

Faith cut into her pizza with a knife. "Hello? I am sitting right here."

"We know," Nick said before picking up his slice, folding it and taking a bite.

Austin set his fork down and copied Nick, losing half his cheese when he took an overly ambitious mouthful. Faith gave him more napkins.

"There are other things you can do," Nick said halfway through his first slice. "You can toss a rubber ball against the side of the house or garage—but only if there aren't any windows."

Which was something he told the kids on his baseball team to do on their own, he thought as they all dived into their dinner. Not that he'd make the mistake of bringing up baseball sign-ups again. Or Austin joining the team.

Nick had just finished his third slice when Faith leaned forward. "That woman has been staring at us since she sat down. Stop," she hissed when he turned. "Don't look."

"Then how am I supposed to see who you mean?"

"Right. Well…be covert about it."

"Covert?"

She nodded at something behind him, presumably the mystery woman. "Use some of your cop tricks so she doesn't see you looking at her."

"I'm not allowed to use the Jedi mind tricks they taught us at the police academy unless there's a high-level security threat." He tossed his crumpled napkin onto his plate and picked up his drink. "Although I could pull out my magic invisibility cloak."

Faith's lips curved. "Fine. Let her see you. She's two tables to your right."

He turned and, sure enough, met Erin Shaffer's eyes. The overweight, middle-aged brunette sat with three women Nick vaguely recognized. But she wasn't paying any attention to whatever had the other women laughing, because Faith had been right—Erin was busy staring at them, blatantly curious.

Seeing she had his attention, Erin wiggled her fingers, which he took to be her version of a flirtatious wave. He lifted his glass to her in a salute, then faced Faith again.

"That's Erin Shaffer," he said. "She's harmless."

"But why is she watching us?" Faith asked in an undertone, still leaning across the table.

He mimicked both her stance and her tone. "Probably because she's already planning her strategy on the best way to spread her latest story all over town."

"What story?"

He couldn't help it. He grinned. "That you and I are together."

CHAPTER SIX

PIZZA CHURNING IN HER stomach, Faith darted her eyes to the other woman. "Together?" she asked hoarsely.

Nick shrugged his broad shoulders. "Yeah. As in a couple."

Austin sat on the edge of the bench seat, his full attention on the teens at the Pac Man game. Still, Faith leaned forward and lowered her voice. "But…but we're not."

"I'm only guessing that's what Erin will say. She might not even be thinking about us at all."

Faith checked again and, sure enough, the woman's attention was still on them. "Can't you do something?"

Nick looked at her as if she'd sniffed way too much hair dye. "Like what? Use a Taser on her for staring at us? Even if she does gossip about us, something new will happen and any rumor about us will die down in a day or two."

Easy for him to say. He wasn't the one trying to keep a low profile.

Sitting back, Faith linked her hands together in her lap. She'd been so intent on getting through the evening, on acting as normal as possible, that she hadn't considered the consequences of being seen with Nick. While there had been the expected initial buzz when she and Austin had moved to town, curiosity had died quickly.

Because they'd faded into the background.

And it wasn't just Erin she had to worry about now. Dozens of people had seen them together, walking down the street, enjoying a meal.

"You okay?" Nick's gaze was intense. As it had been when he'd asked her about Serenity Springs. As if he was searching for something.

"I…I don't like to be gossiped about," Faith said lamely. "Besides, won't a rumor like that hurt your reputation?"

His lips twitched. "I think my rep as a carefree bachelor will survive."

Ducking her head, she viciously twisted the paper napkin in her lap. Of course Nick would survive. To him, it was harmless chitchat.

A group of boys Austin's age raced past the booth on their way to the video games.

"Whoa," Nick said, pulling the last one onto the seat next to him. "If your mom finds out you were running through a restaurant like that, she'll shave your head."

The boy crossed his arms over his sandy-colored curls. "No way. I'm growing it out."

"You grow it much more," Nick said, nudging the boy with his elbow, "you won't be able to fit a ball cap on it. This is my sister Kathleen's son, Trevor," he told Faith. "Trev, this is Ms. Lewis—she works for Aunt Britney—and her son, Austin."

"Nice to meet you," Trevor said with a grin that showed off his braces. He turned to Austin. "Hey."

"Hi," Austin mumbled, staring at his shoes.

"What are you doing here?" Nick asked. "Besides causing trouble?"

"It's Josh's birthday so we're going to have pizza and then sleep out in his backyard. And I bet Matthew five bucks I could beat him at Donkey Kong."

"Well, you'd better get to it."

Before Trevor could slide out of the seat, Faith caught Nick giving his nephew a pointed look, then nodding his head ever so slightly at Austin. Her heart lodged in her throat at the simple, sweet gesture.

When they'd first arrived in Kingsville, she'd tried to get Austin to make friends, encouraged him to invite kids from school over to their house or to attend after-school activities, but he'd been so against it she'd backed off. She'd never stopped hoping he would come out of his shell.

Or stopped worrying that her fears, her choices were the reason he'd built that shell in the first place.

"Hey, Austin, you want to come, too?" Trevor asked, as polite and charming as his uncle.

"No." Austin jumped to his feet and turned to Faith. "Can we leave now?"

She opened her mouth, only to shut it again. Reprimanding him about his lack of manners in front of a boy his own age certainly wouldn't help matters.

"The guys are waiting for me, Uncle Nick," Trevor said quietly.

"You'd better go then. I'll see you at practice next week."

"Nice to meet you." He tossed the words over his shoulder to Faith as he took off.

Something in Faith burned as she watched Trevor join his friends while her son stood alone, his face set, his hands fisted at his sides. "It's not that late," she said gently. "If you want to play some more, you can."

"I don't. I just want to go home."

"Honey…" She reached for him, but he stepped back and she dropped her hand. "We'll leave as soon as I pay the bill."

"I'm going to wait outside."

She almost told him no. That she wanted him to wait with her where she could see he was safe, but she noticed him trying to blink away tears.

"That's fine." After all, it was still light out and she had a clear view of the sidewalk. "I'll be right out."

"He okay?" Nick asked after Austin left.

No. He should be over with the other boys, joining in on their laughter and horseplay. Austin used to be so outgoing. Friendly. Until they left Serenity Springs. Now he was someone she barely recognized. Having her son was the one thing, the only thing, she'd ever done right, and she was somehow messing it up. Making everything worse.

"He's fine," she croaked, swallowing the tears clogging her throat. Sliding out of the booth, she dug into her purse for her wallet. "Just…tired probably. He was up late last night."

Nick picked up the bill the waiter had left. "Why don't you let me get this? That way you can go out with him."

She snatched it from him. "This is my treat, remember?"

Nick stuck his hands into his front pockets. "Not your treat. More like your way of repaying me so you don't feel as if you owe me. So you don't have to wonder if *I* feel as if you owe me." Their waiter, carrying a tray of salads, walked past them, forcing Nick to step closer to Faith. "Or what I may want from you in return."

Pressure built in her chest until she couldn't take a full breath. He must be a better cop than she'd realized. And that was something she couldn't afford to forget again.

"It's my treat," she repeated firmly, but since the hand holding the check trembled, she hid it behind her back. "And my way of thanking you for your help with the water heater."

He studied her for a long moment before inclining his head. "My mistake. Why don't I go out and wait with Austin." And then he went outside.

They walked back to her house in awkward silence. Austin rode next to them slowly, both wheels firmly on the road, his eyes straight ahead. At the end of their block, he sped up so that by the time she and Nick reached her house, he was already on the front porch, waiting to be let inside.

Faith hurried up the steps and handed Austin the box of leftover pizza so she could dig through her purse for her house keys. The moment she'd unlocked the door he rushed past her.

"Please put the pizza in the fridge," she called.

"'Kay," he muttered from inside.

"Night, Austin," Nick said.

A door slammed.

"I'm so sorry," she said in a rush. "I'm not sure what's gotten into that boy."

"Like you said, he must be overtired."

"Tired or not, there's no excuse for being so rude." Nibbling her cheek, she glanced anxiously inside. When she turned back, Nick had edged closer.

She gasped, then tried to cover it by faking a yawn. "Sorry. I guess I'm…more tired than I realized."

One corner of his mouth quirked up. "It's barely nine o'clock."

"Yes, well, I had to get up early…." She reached behind her, felt the doorknob and almost wilted in relief. Her stomach fluttered, her palms grew damp. For God's sake, she used to wrap men around her little finger, used to get whatever she wanted by batting her eyelashes. And now she couldn't even stand on her own front porch with one.

It was pathetic.

And after spending a few hours in Nick's company it was way too easy to forget she wasn't an ordinary single mom spending time with her son and a very nice, attractive man. But if Austin's behavior tonight had proved one thing, it was that she needed to keep her focus. On her son. And their secrets.

"Thanks again for all your help. I guess I'll see you around sometime."

In the twilight, his teeth flashed in a quick grin. "I'm sure you will."

Before she could make it into the safety of her house, Nick reached behind her. Faith froze, her breath trapped in her lungs, as he gently pulled the door shut.

"What—what are you doing?"

"Now, you see, the thing is, I've never walked a pretty woman to her door without kissing her good-night." He seemed amused. "I don't want to break that tradition."

She pressed back against the door. "All good things must come to an end."

"True. But not tonight."

He leaned down and she slapped both hands against his chest. Felt his heart under her fingers, the pace of it steady and strong. And a far cry from her own erratic beating. "This wasn't a real date," she squeaked.

"It doesn't have to mean anything, Faith," he said, his breath stirring the loose tendrils of hair by her ear. "It's just a kiss. Just to keep my streak alive."

Still smiling, he slowly closed the distance between them. She kept her eyes on his as he brushed his mouth against hers. By God, if she was going to be kissed by a man for the first time in over four years, she was damn well going to do it with her eyes open.

He kept his arms at his sides while he kissed her again, his touch as soft as the evening breeze. When he eased back, his smile was gone. Her knees were weak. Her nerve endings tingled. A longing to lean into him, to just…be held by him, filled her. But only because she hadn't been with a man in so long. Because she felt so alone sometimes.

He lowered his head toward her again, his eyes dark.

"Night," she blurted, before slipping inside and quietly shutting the door on him.

Her heart pounding, she leaned back, her head hitting the wall with a solid thump. Though that brief encounter could barely even qualify as a kiss, she still tasted him. She pressed her lips together. Hearing his footsteps, she reached for the curtain and peeked out in time to watch him walk to his car.

He didn't look back.

She didn't want him to. There was no reason. Obviously, what had happened hadn't concerned him, so why should she let it stress her? Shutting off the porch light, she made her way through her dark house up the stairs. This time things would work out for her and Austin. As long as she continued to fool everyone, they'd be safe. As for Nick? Well, after the way she'd just shot him down, she doubted she'd have to worry about him anymore.

THUMP. THUMP. THUMP.

Faith cringed as she took down the last pair of Austin's underwear from the makeshift clothesline she'd constructed in the backyard. Austin sure had taken Nick's advice to heart. Ever since Nick gave him ideas on how to improve his coordination, he hadn't touched his video-game system. A fact she was grateful for, truly. But now her son spent every last waking minute bouncing a tennis ball against the side of the house. The constant *thump, thump, thump* was driving her crazy.

And if he broke a window, she was sending the bill to Nick.

Thunder rumbled softly in the distance as Faith set the full laundry basket on the back steps. The evening air was thick with the threat of rain. They were due for a storm later. Quickening her pace, she crossed the yard and unhooked one end of the plastic-coated rope, which she wound around her arm as she walked back to the house, hanging it on a hook by the door.

She picked up the basket. "Time to go in, Austin."

He neatly caught the tennis ball with one hand. "Ten more minutes?"

"That's what you said ten minutes ago."

He seemed to consider this. "Five more minutes?" he asked, his tone ever hopeful.

"Sure. Five minutes." He whooped and tossed the ball again. She hunched her shoulders against the sound. "As in," she continued, "if you're not in the shower in five minutes, your bedtime for the week will be seven o'clock. And you need to be quick because we're supposed to get a thunderstorm."

"Aww, Mom."

"Aww, Austin."

His head hanging, he marched past her into the house.

She tipped her face to the gray sky and inhaled deeply. Peace. Glorious peace. *Thank you, God.*

Pushing open the door with her free hand, she maneuvered herself and the laundry inside.

It'd been three days since they'd gone out for pizza, and she hadn't seen or heard from Nick since.

The shower turned on as she reached the top of the stairs. She went into her bedroom and set the basket on her twin-size bed. Any worries that Nick had a thing for her were baseless. Not to mention egotistical. Just because he'd asked her out before and then kissed her hardly meant the man was enraptured with her. And his not contacting her was a huge relief.

Although you'd think that when you bought a guy dinner and let him kiss you, he could at least have the courtesy to call.

Huffing out a breath, she began to fold clothes and set them in neat piles. It didn't matter if Nick ever spoke to her again. It'd be best if he didn't. He obviously believed the story she'd told him about her past, and most importantly, her marriage. If they were to…socialize he might want to get to know her even better. Since she scarcely knew herself anymore, that couldn't happen.

Picking up the piles of Austin's underwear and socks, she went into his room. She put the clean clothes in his dresser, went back for his T-shirts and noticed the shower had shut off.

She knocked on the bathroom door. "Did you wash your hair?"

The water started again.

It must've been the quickest hair washing on record because not three minutes later, Austin came into his room.

"It's not even dark outside," he complained, his hair a wet mass hanging in his face, the baggy Spiderman boxers that had fit him perfectly when she'd bought them not six months ago now two inches too short. "Why did I have to come in?"

"Because you've been bouncing that ball against the house for over an hour. Give me a break, would you?" She crossed to the end of the bed for the last T-shirt, her foot catching on something. "What's this?" Pulling the wide black strap off her foot, she slid Austin's Transformers' backpack out from under the bed. Grunted at its unexpected weight. "I thought you lost this."

"Don't!" Austin snatched the bag from her. "That's my stuff."

"First of all, you need to settle down *and* watch your tone. Secondly, I wasn't trying to take your stuff. But if this bag is so important to you, why is it under the bed? And why did you tell me it was lost?"

He hugged it to his chest and shrugged.

Something was definitely going on here. "Come on…" Sitting on the bed, she patted the mattress beside her. "Let's talk about this."

He didn't raise his head. "It's just some stuff I like to keep packed. So when you asked me why I wasn't using it for school, I said I lost it. Because I need to keep it under my bed."

"Can I see?" She held out her hand. After a long moment, Austin slowly gave her the backpack. "Thanks."

She unzipped the bag and began emptying it. By the time she was done, she had a sizable pile of some of Austin's favorite things, including two *Captain Underpants* books, four Lego kits, at least a dozen Matchbox cars, the remote control Jeep she'd bought him for his birthday and his new X-Men comic book.

"Honey," she said, "I don't understand. What is all of this?"

"I'm tired of leaving all my stuff behind when we have to move," he said softly.

"But if you keep it packed, you can't play with any of these things. Wouldn't it be better to—"

"No." He shook his hair out of his face. "I don't care if I can't play with them. This way I can get them. I don't have to leave them behind."

Oh, God. It was as if someone had taken a baseball bat to her stomach. Faith bent forward and tried to catch her breath. This was her fault. All her fault. She was constantly uprooting him, forcing him to lie and live on the run.

Worse was how she'd ignored all the signs and symptoms. How she'd hoped time would heal Austin's wounds. No wonder he'd gotten so upset when Nick had mentioned baseball sign-ups. Austin figured they wouldn't be in town long so why bother trying out for the team? Why bother making friends when he'd have to leave them.

He was protecting himself when *she* should be the one protecting him. The one making him feel loved and safe, yes, but also secure. He deserved that. He deserved more than what she was doing to him.

Faith smoothed a hand over his damp hair. "You can unpack the bag. Use your stuff. We're not going anywhere."

The look on his face made it clear he didn't believe her. "You said that about Serenity Springs."

"You're right, but this time…" This time what? *She meant it. She promised.* Words. Nothing but empty words that were far from enough to convince Austin she was telling the truth. Besides, if they were found, they would have to run again. And she couldn't lie to her son.

She tugged on his hand and he shuffled forward until he was in front of her. "I want you to listen to me." She waited for him to meet her eyes. "I understand this hasn't been easy. It hasn't been easy on either one of us, but no matter how much we both wanted to stay in Serenity Springs, we couldn't."

"Because that guy was looking for us."

"Right." Her stomach churned as she remembered how they'd almost been caught two years ago, when a private investigator had tracked them to the small town in upstate New York. How close they'd come to being sent back to their old life. Well, Austin would've been sent back. She most likely would have ended up in prison.

"It wasn't easy for you to leave," she said, "I get that. You had friends and had fun on the basketball team, but it wasn't safe for us there anymore."

"Why can't he leave us alone?"

He. Austin's father. She squeezed his hand. "I don't know, baby."

"It's because of me, isn't it?" he asked in a ragged whisper. "He wants me back."

Feeling sick, she nodded. "But I'm not going to let him take you from me. I'm not going to let him—or anyone else—hurt you. I promise."

He wrapped his thin arms around her neck and held on tight. "Okay," he said into her neck, his words muffled.

Faith breathed in his clean scent and forgot her fears and all her mistakes. Just for a second. Long enough to imprint this moment on her brain, in her memory. The weight of her son's head on her shoulder, the feel of his cool, damp hair against her cheek. The improbable, impossible sense that as long as she held on to him, everything would be all right.

He stepped out of her arms. "Do I have to unpack my bag?"

"Not if you don't want to," she said slowly, unwilling to take such a small comfort away from him. Thunder rumbled, closer this time. She forced a smile. "Why don't we have a no-TV night tonight?"

"Can we finish *Hatchet?*"

They had at least one hundred pages of the classic Gary Paulson book to go. "Sure. I'm not working tomorrow so we can both sleep in."

Austin pumped his fist. "Yes!"

"Get the book and meet me in the living room. I'll make some popcorn."

Faith picked up the laundry basket and trudged down the stairs. Alone in the kitchen, she gripped the edge of the sink as she battled tears.

She filled a glass with water and gulped it down, using both hands to hold the glass steady. She had to get ahold of herself. Had to be strong. Smart. And, God help her, she had to be devious.

Her husband held all the cards, always had. He would never stop searching for them. She'd been fooling herself to think she could run from him forever. It was only a matter of time, but he would catch up to them—as he had in Serenity Springs. Luckily, quick thinking and quicker actions had saved them. When—if—he got close to them again, she needed to make sure he couldn't take Austin.

And to do that, she needed help. She couldn't do this on her own. Not any longer.

Her fingers tightened on the glass and she carefully set it down before she gave in to the urge to heave it across the room. Lightning flashed, followed a few seconds later by a loud clap of thunder. Rain suddenly poured from the sky as if someone had turned on a faucet.

Staring blindly out the window, Faith chewed on her thumbnail. One thing she'd learned was that having the right connections meant the difference between success and failure.

With well-connected, powerful people in her corner, she could finally stand up to her husband. She could stop running. She needed someone, someone strong and honorable and protective of those he loved. And she knew the perfect person.

She needed Nick Coletti.

CHAPTER SEVEN

"HEY, COLETTI," fellow officer Martin Hill said late Monday morning as he walked up to Nick's desk at the police station, "someone here to see you."

Nick looked up from the keyboard he'd been pecking away at, and then frowned. "Faith? What are you doing here?"

She smiled tremulously and lifted the hand holding a closed umbrella in a wave. "Hi."

He stood as Marty walked away, and Faith's smile faded.

"Is this a bad time?" she asked, adjusting the strap of her purse on her shoulder. "It is, isn't it? I'm sorry to drop by like this. I…I should've called or something. I can come back…."

He rounded his desk and caught her by the elbow before she could take off. "No. Sorry, I'm just…" He shook his head. "Sorry. Now's fine."

"Oh. Good." He followed her nervous glance around the room and noticed his coworkers watching them.

"How about a cup of coffee?" he suggested, guiding her out of the large room with his hand on her lower back. Surprisingly, though she tensed, she didn't pull away.

There was something…different about her today. Her hair was the same—loose and wavy to her shoulders—but she'd smudged her eyes with color, making them seem bigger, and her lips were a glossy pink. And while he wouldn't classify her light brown pants and loose white shirt sexy by any means, at least they weren't two sizes too big. And the top had a wide neck that showed her collarbones, which was for some crazy reason as sexy to him as if she'd had on a low-cut top.

Once inside the small break room, he shut the door. "Have a seat," he said, crossing to the coffeepot on the counter. "Chief makes the coffee pretty strong so I suggest you add something to cut it back to only slightly toxic."

"Creamer's good. Thanks." She set her purse down on the scarred wooden table and sat on the edge of a metal chair. She reached to put her umbrella underneath.

He poured two cups of coffee and added a hefty amount of powdered creamer to both. Sitting opposite Faith, he placed one cup in front of her. "Everything okay?"

"Huh? Oh, yeah. Fine." She sipped her coffee, made a face and quickly put the cup back down. "I'm off today. From the salon."

"I know where you work, Faith," he said. Since nothing was wrong, he leaned back and drank his coffee. Hell, he might as well let her tell him what she wanted in her own time. It wasn't as if he had anything more pressing to deal with than filling out arrest reports. Until a call came in.

She dropped her gaze. "Right. I...actually, I came to give you something." She hauled her bag onto her lap and, after a moment digging through it, handed him an object wrapped in a red-and-white-checked dishcloth. "You must've left this behind when you fixed the water heater."

He unwrapped it. "I appreciate you coming down here on your day off, but this isn't mine."

She frowned prettily. "Really? Maybe it's Ethan's?"

Nick held up the tarnished brass tool. It was as long as his hand, flat and light, with a long notch cut out of its center. "I don't think it's Ethan's, either. Unless he's taken up lobstering."

"Excuse me?"

"It's a lobster measure. Far as I know, Ethan doesn't do any lobstering."

"Austin found it in the basement last night and I thought it was yours..."

Grinning, Nick tapped the end of the tool on the table. "So you didn't bring this in as an excuse to see me again after blowing me off the other night?"

She blinked several times. "I—I didn't... I mean...of course not."

Well, well. Maybe his teasing hadn't been all that far off base. "Why don't I ask Ethan if he's missing this? Maybe he's gotten tired of golf and has taken up a new hobby."

"I didn't blow you off," she said as he stood.

"You shut the door in my face," he reminded her.

"I said good-night first." She wrapped her hands around her cup, then looked up at him from under her eyelashes. "You haven't called me."

He narrowed his eyes at her chiding, flirtatious tone. "I didn't think you wanted me to." To test her, he added, "If you wanted to talk to me, you could've gotten hold of me at any time."

"I was going to," she stated, so quickly he knew it was a lie. Especially when she said it to the table. "I meant to, it's just that I was busy. With work. And Austin, of course." Reaching for the dishcloth, she smoothed out the wrinkles before folding it. "I would've called you yesterday," she continued, folding the cloth again, "but I had so much laundry to do and then it rained...."

"It's still raining. And yet here you are."

She sighed and slumped in her seat. "I need your help."

Why hadn't she just said that in the first place? That pride of hers was an almost tangible thing. He set his coffee down and gripped the back of the chair. "What's up?"

"Does that offer to help Austin get on the baseball team still stand?"

"He said he wasn't interested."

"He was. He is. I think he's nervous about being the new kid. I guess I hadn't realized how much his... shyness...was affecting him until the other night, when he wouldn't even go with your nephew to play video games."

"I can appreciate you wanting Austin to break out of

his shell," Nick said, "but if he's not interested in baseball, forcing him to join the team might backfire."

"That's just it," she said, leaning forward so far that her shirt caught on the edge of the table, pulling the material down. Averting his eyes as she tugged it back into place, he gulped down more coffee to ease the sudden dryness in his mouth. "Austin loves baseball. He's been doing those drills you told him about every free minute, and he follows the games on TV. Plus he scours the sports section of the newspaper every morning at the salon."

"I'm not sure what I can do," Nick admitted. "We've already started practicing."

Faith stood and rounded the table toward him with a slow, sensual sway of her hips. He'd never seen her walk that way before. Laying her hand on his forearm, she tilted her head so that her hair slid over her shoulder. "I'd be so grateful if you could help us out."

The soft, lyrical tone of her voice reminded him of the South. Her hand was warm and she traced tiny circles on his arm with her forefinger, while ever so subtly pressing close enough so that if he moved, he'd brush against her breasts.

Nick stood stock-still, his jaw clenched.

Something was way off here. He'd had women come on to him before—plenty of times. Some flirted in an attempt to get out of a ticket. Some wanted him in their bed. But Faith? What could she want from him?

"Yeah?" he asked huskily. "How grateful?"

She swallowed, but the determination in her face didn't waver. Neither did her eyes from his. While his instincts told him she might not like acting the part of a woman willing to use her body to get what she wanted, she wasn't new to it, either.

And what in the hell was that about?

She moved her hand farther up his arm, her short nails gently scratching him. "Grateful enough to repay you. However you want." But she couldn't hide the slight tremor in her voice or the tightness around her mouth.

"What I want," he said quietly, "is for you not to insult either of us any more than you already have."

Her brows drew together as she removed her hand from his arm. "What?"

Nick strode to the door because, damn it, he'd been tempted to take what she'd been offering. And that was wrong on so many levels, not the least of which being that when he'd kissed her a few days ago she couldn't get away fast enough.

"Wait," she called, stopping him at the door. "Where are you going?"

"Back to work." He squeezed the doorknob. "I'll put in a call to the baseball league's president. I'm sure once I explain the situation, he'll let Austin join the team. If the rain lets up, we'll have practice tonight at six at Case Field. Have Austin there half an hour early so you can fill out the necessary paperwork."

Then he walked away.

THE BASEBALL SAILED toward her. Faith squealed and cowered, covering her face with her arms as it bounced a few feet from her and rolled past, hitting the chain-link fence around the sunken dugout before landing in a puddle.

"Mom," Austin said in disgust, "you're supposed to catch it. I didn't even throw it hard that time."

"I'm doing the best I can, Austin." Well, as best as she wanted, anyway. She didn't have some secret yen to be in the NBA or wherever it was baseball players played.

The rain had let up and Faith had brought Austin to the baseball field after an early supper. Jogging through the wet, spongy grass to the ball, she grabbed it, wound up and threw it as hard as she could. Once again her aim was off, and instead of arcing toward Austin, it went left. Her son raced over, dived and caught it in his glove as he slid across the outfield in his brand-new, had-to-have-them-today-so-she-paid-full-price-for-them baseball pants.

"Do you have any idea how hard it is to get grass stains out of white pants?" she asked, but Austin couldn't hear her over his self-congratulatory whooping. The only reason they'd bought white was because that was the last pair the small sports store had in Austin's size.

"Bleach should get them clean," a deep, familiar voice said.

Her heart stopped for a moment. Nick walked toward her, carrying a large duffel bag over one shoulder and some folders and a large binder under his other arm. The baseball cap he was wearing backward made him appear somewhat younger. But no less intimidating.

"Nice dive," Nick told Austin as he tossed the huge bag into the dugout.

Austin grinned, his own ball cap covering his entire forehead. "Thanks. Okay, Mom, here comes another one."

He threw the ball, a hard-liner right at her. Though she wanted to squeak and drop to the ground—stains be damned—Faith held her gloved hand out and prayed the stupid ball wouldn't hit her. Again.

It was whizzing toward her when suddenly a hand appeared in her line of vision and caught it.

"You hold your glove like that," Nick said evenly, "and the ball's going to catch the tip of it and hit your face. You need to hold the glove up—" he pulled her hand back "—like this so you can catch the ball in the pocket. Pop fly," he called, before tossing the ball into the air. Austin raced after it. "And it might help," Nick added, "if you kept your eyes open."

"They *were* open," Faith insisted. She let her arm drop to her side. "Thank you for saving my nose. But didn't catching the ball like that hurt your hand?"

He flexed his fingers. "Stings like a son of a bitch."

Trevor raced onto the field, hauling a bag almost as big as the one Nick had carried, a bat with a mitt on its handle slung over his shoulder. He wore gray baseball pants—at least Faith hoped they were supposed to be gray and hadn't started out white—a T-shirt with the sleeves cut off, revealing his skinny arms, and a muddy pair of cleats. His ball cap had a bent rim, at least an inch of grime, and barely covered his curls.

"Want me to help Austin warm up, Uncle Nick?" Trevor asked when he reached them.

"That'd be great," Nick said. Trevor dropped the bag, slid his mitt off the bat and joined Austin in the outfield.

Faith took off the glove Britney had lent her and wiped her sweaty palm down the side of her jeans. "Now that you've taught me the proper way to catch, maybe next time you could show me how to throw. I'm afraid Austin is losing patience chasing after the ball."

"I'm sure he appreciates that you're trying, even if the end results aren't all that great. And if he doesn't, he will someday."

"So your mom throws like a girl, too?" Faith asked, hoping to get him to smile. To get him to forget the way she'd made a complete ass of herself with him earlier at the police station.

He glanced at her. "My mom didn't play catch with me."

"I'd just assumed…"

"After my dad died, she couldn't get out of bed for three months, let alone take care of five kids." He picked up the bag Trevor had dropped. "When the worst of her grief passed she was too busy trying to keep us all clothed and fed to play games."

"Is that why you had to take care of your sisters?"

He sent her a sharp look.

"I heard…well, Britney mentioned you helped raise her…." What had he said when he'd defended his paying Austin to run to the hardware store for him? *You think I don't understand what it's like for Austin, sitting here while you work?*

Faith had no doubt now that Nick did understand.

He shrugged, uncomfortable either with her question or the subject as a whole. "I did what I had to do."

"How old were you?"

"Eleven."

Eleven? Dear Lord, that was only two years older than Austin. Faith couldn't imagine her son having so much responsibility thrust upon him, and she couldn't stop her heart from going out to Nick, to the little boy who'd had to take on so much at such a young age. No wonder he was so protective of his sisters. He'd spent most of his life caring for them.

"You'll need to fill out a couple of forms," Nick said. "The waiver for insurance purposes will have to be signed before he can participate in a practice with us, but the others can wait until later."

"I can fill them out now," she said slowly, following his abrupt change of subject. "It's no problem."

He nodded.

Faith followed Nick into the dugout. He set his folder on the bench and leafed through the papers, not giving her a second glance. She couldn't help noticing how standoffish he was being.

Finally, he straightened and handed her some forms. "The top one is the release." He gave her a pen and gestured to the bench. "You can fill them out in here before the rest of the team shows up. Just leave them and the check in that top folder."

"Check? You have to pay to join the baseball team?" That seemed sort of…un-American somehow.

"Aren't you the one who lives by the belief that nothing's free?"

"Ouch," she whispered. No doubt about it, he was still angry with her about her come-on.

He took his hat off and raked his free hand through his hair. "Sorry." Slapping the cap against his thigh, he added, "The registration fee helps cover the cost of insurance for the kids, plus equipment. Between our local fundraiser and the money from the concessions during games, we make enough to buy the uniforms and have a picnic at the end of the season. But if you can't swing it at this time—"

"I can. And I want to thank you for allowing Austin to play."

Nick settled his hat back on his head. "I didn't have a full roster so it's no big deal."

The sound of her son's laughter drifted to her. "Maybe not to you, but to Austin it is a big deal." Inhaling a fortifying breath, Faith skimmed a finger over the back of Nick's hand. "And to me."

He stepped back and she curled her fingers into her palm. "All I did was call Bill Snyder, the president of the league, and explain the situation to him."

Faith winced at Nick's cool, dismissive tone. She'd really made a mess of things. The best thing to do, the smart thing, would be to let it go. Give him a few days.

"Practice is over at eight," he said, picking up a large mitt and turning to leave. "You're welcome to stay and watch."

"I'm sorry."

His shoulders tensed. "For what?"

She crossed her arms and glanced at the boys to make sure they weren't within hearing distance. "For what happened earlier. At the police station."

Two long strides and Nick stood before her. "You mean when you offered to do whatever I wanted in exchange for me getting Austin on the team? Tell me, Faith, what if I'd taken you up on it?" His eyes glittered and his mouth was an angry slash. "What if I'd said the price for my help was that I wanted you in my bed?"

"I...I wouldn't have..."

"I know you don't think much of me—"

"That's not true!" she said, appalled.

"—but I hadn't realized you actually believed I was the type of guy to take advantage of someone in that way. What really bugs the hell out of me is you thinking so little of yourself that you'd make the offer in the first place."

She winced. "That wasn't... I don't feel that way. About either of us."

But she had thought about herself that way once upon a time. Had thought all she could offer a man were her looks, her sex appeal and her performance in bed. She'd kept men interested by becoming who they wanted her to be. She'd used men, yes, but it was only recently that she'd realized how she'd allowed herself to be used in return.

"I'm sorry," she repeated. "It was a huge error in judgment on my part. I'm not even sure what I was thinking."

"I'm not that guy, Faith."

Her heart raced. "Wha-what guy?"

"Your ex-husband or whoever it was who hurt you. I'm not him," Nick said, enunciating each word. "So if you ever want my help, just ask me." He leaned forward, his dark eyes hooded. "But don't ever try to play me again."

After he left, Faith slumped on the bench and let her head fall back against the stone wall. Then she thought about all of the dirt and grime on the wall and quickly sat up. So much for her brilliant plan to befriend Nick in the hopes of getting him to care about her and Austin. To protect them. What better person to have in her corner than a well-respected cop? Sure, it was risky, but she had to believe Nick wouldn't arrest her, or worse, send Austin back to his father, if he found out the truth.

Not once he discovered what her husband had done.

But she was blowing it.

She'd been so focused on getting what she wanted, she'd forgotten the number one rule she used to live by: know your target.

Elbows on her knees, she rested her head in her hands. Nick had a strong sense of honor and he didn't use women. He respected them. Maybe because he'd been raised by a single mom, and had one sister who was a single mother, as well. He took his responsibilities to those he cared about seriously, and as cop, had devoted his life to taking care of the town he obviously loved.

She watched him throw the ball first to Austin and then to Trevor, offering guidance and words of praise in equal measure. He was patient. Loyal. And because all that made him sound like a harmless puppy, when his anger at her today had proved he was anything but,

CHAPTER EIGHT

A WEEK LATER, Faith set her folded sweatshirt on the bottom wooden bleacher before sitting on it. She searched the crowded field, relaxing when she spotted Austin warming up with Trevor and the only girl on the team, a redheaded pixie named Melyssa. When Faith and Austin had gotten in the car to come to today's practice, he'd told her she didn't have to stay, but she'd convinced him she enjoyed watching him. She hoped he continued to believe that was the only reason she sat on the hard bleachers for two hours, three times a week, and not because she wasn't ready to leave him alone yet.

Some days she doubted she'd ever be ready.

Shielding her eyes from the sun with her hand, she scanned the field for Nick. Just to see if he was there. It wasn't as if she sought him out at every practice. She pursed her lips and lowered her hand as she spied him at the opening in the fence by first base, talking with Melyssa's mother, a long-legged strawberry blonde.

Okay, so maybe Faith did seek him out. Ever since that first practice, when he'd been upset with her, she'd been trying to get them back to where they'd been before she'd miscalculated and come on to him at the police station. And she'd finally made some progress.

As if sensing her watching him, Nick lifted his head and met her eyes. While he didn't smile, he no longer scowled at her every time he saw her, either. And he even lifted a hand in a wave, causing the blonde to glance over her shoulder to see who had stolen his attention.

Faith waved in response, but Nick was speaking to the blonde again. Whatever he said must have been hilarious because she tipped her head back—the better to show off her long, graceful neck—and laughed, a deep throaty sound that had both of the assistant coaches glancing her way. Then she laid her hand on Nick's arm, pressing her slim body oh-so-subtly against his. Nothing overt. Nothing that would draw the attention of the kids or tip off the few adults who helped with the team, but Faith knew all the moves.

Heck, she'd perfected the moves in high school.

The blonde was interested in Nick. And since he didn't set her away and glower at her—as he'd done with Faith at the police station—it looked as if he might be interested, too.

Faith felt a twinge of jealousy but she shoved it aside. Not her concern, she told herself as she raised her book and looked blindly at the words before her. It wasn't as if she really wanted Nick for herself.

But she couldn't fault the other woman for her taste in men, either. By all appearances, Nick was a prime catch. Not only was he honorable, but he went above and beyond for his family and friends. He was patient with Austin and the other boys on the team, never raising his voice and always giving positive reinforcement. And last practice, when one of the fathers yelled at his son over a missed catch, Nick had stepped in and made it clear in that low-key way of his that he wouldn't tolerate anyone berating the kids for any reason.

If she didn't know better, Faith would think he was too good to be true.

She snorted. No man was that wonderful. Hadn't she thought her husband was the man of her dreams? Part of it—what had initially drawn her to him—had been his wealth, yes. But she'd also been impressed by his philanthropy and how he'd reached out to underprivileged children.

Until she'd learned the real reason why he set up the after-school programs for inner city youth. How it fed his sickness.

I'm not that guy. Nick's voice floated through her mind. Her fingers tightened, bending the cover of the book back. No, he wasn't her husband, but that didn't mean she could trust him.

"That's my favorite author." The willowy blonde who'd been talking with Nick blocked the sun as she sat down next to Faith. "That's a great romance, and wait until you read the second in the series. Pure magic. I'm a sucker for a happy ending." She grinned and motioned to Nick. "And there's a guy who would be perfect hero material."

Faith stared at the woman. "Excuse me?"

The blonde laughed. "If you haven't noticed, you're about the only woman in town who hasn't. I'm Tracy, by the way," she added, smiling and holding out her hand.

Faith closed the book and set it on her lap before shaking Tracy's hand. "Faith Lewis."

"Nice to meet you. Nick suggested I ask if you'd be interested in volunteering to work the concession stand for a few of the home games."

"I've never worked a—"

Tracy waved her hand. "It's easy. I'll schedule you to work with me. I've been running it for the past two years. How about the first game, next Friday?"

"Uh…sure. I guess that's okay."

"Great. Let me put you on the schedule." Tracy took a paper and pen out of her purse and wrote Faith's name on a spreadsheet.

Instead of going on her way, Tracy then crossed her long, toned legs—showcased perfectly in a pair of bright green shorts. "You haven't been in town long, have you?"

"A few months," Faith replied, feeling like a hot mess next to this woman with her cute halter top and expertly applied makeup. Faith pulled her shoulders back, but not even excellent posture could make her look better in her baggy capri pants and boxy top. It was times like this that she wondered if she was biting off her nose to spite her face.

Nick called the kids together at the pitcher's mound. "He's so great with them, isn't he?" Tracy commented with a sigh.

Faith made a noncommittal sound.

"I heard you two were seeing each other."

"What?" Faith gaped at her. "No. I mean, we went out. Nick, Austin and I went out for pizza. But that was just a…friendly dinner."

"So you're not involved?"

Faith had to bite the inside of her cheek to stop herself from snapping that her and Nick's relationship—or lack thereof—wasn't any of Tracy's business. But that would be playing right into the woman's hands. She was fishing for information, sizing Faith up, seeing if she was competition.

"Nick and I are…" What? Friends? Not even close. "We hardly know each other," she answered honestly.

"That's too bad," Tracy said, the calculation in her eyes belying her words. "Well, I'd better get going." She rose to her feet. "I have to pick up a few groceries before practice ends. I'll see you next Friday."

Tracy sauntered past the dugout, trailing her fingers along the chain-link fence behind home plate, where Nick was tossing the ball into the air and hitting it to the kids in the field. She said something that had him grinning in response.

Her stomach churning, Faith went back to her book. Why shouldn't Tracy be interested in Nick? He deserved a woman who wasn't afraid to be seen with him, and who trusted him with her child. Who didn't have secrets that could jeopardize his career. He deserved better than a woman who only wanted to use him for her own personal gain.

He deserved so much better than her.

NICK PRESSED HIS PALMS against his gritty eyes. "You can't go eight months without balancing your checkbook."

"Why not?" Britney asked as she touched up her makeup at one of the stations in the salon. "There's plenty of money in there, isn't there?"

"That's not the point." He tilted his head to one side, cracking his neck. As soon as he'd finished his shift at work, he'd come over to the salon, not even taking time to change out of his uniform. For the past two hours, he'd been hunched over the mess that was Brit's Snips's finances, breathing shallowly so as not to inhale too much of the toxic scents in the air. "You have to take your business seriously," he continued. "If you can't handle the bookkeeping, you need to hire it out."

She faced him, a tube of lipstick in her hand, a quizzical expression on her face. "Why would I hire someone when you can do it for me?"

Why indeed.

Faith came into the room from the back, carrying a broom. Not even giving them a glance, she began sweeping up the cut hair from her last customer.

Nick lifted an envelope. "This bill from J. H. Thompson says it's the third notice for hair supplies. Didn't you pay them last month?"

Applying the lipstick, Britney shrugged.

Where was the panic she'd displayed earlier when she'd called him at work, telling him her favorite supplier had threatened to shut her off? Where were the tears and pleas for help that she'd shown when he'd first arrived and stared, dumbfounded, at the piles of paper-work—bills, both paid and unpaid. Invoices and orders and receipts. He'd even come across a torn copy of Brit's New Year's resolutions.

First on the list had been Get Organized.

"You can't ignore this and hope it goes away," he said. "Now come over here so—"

A motorcycle engine revved outside, vibrating the floor.

Britney whirled around. "There's Michael!" She tossed the lipstick into her tiny purse, snapped it shut and gave herself a last once-over in the mirror. She must've decided her shorts were indeed short enough and her top cut low enough, because she tossed her curly hair and grinned. "I'll see you both later."

"What?" Nick stood so fast his chair flew back and banged into the wall. "Where the hell do you think you're going?"

Britney stopped at the door. "Didn't I tell you?" she asked, all big-eyed innocence, as if she was still seven and could wrap him around her finger. "Michael and I are taking a ride along the coast and then having a romantic picnic on the beach. He suggested it for our two-month anniversary. Isn't that so sweet?"

"Adorable. Too bad you need to stay here and get your checkbook straightened out."

The motorcycle's engine revved again. Brit's lower lip stuck out in a pout. "But, Nicky, I can't. Michael has had this planned for days. I can't disappoint him."

The headache he'd been fighting since he'd sat down

to clean up her mess intensified. "Then why did you ask me to come over?"

"I didn't think it would take this long. Why don't you just leave it and I'll look at it again tomorrow? I'm sure once I've had a chance to talk to Gene, the salesman at Thompson, everything will be all right." She hurried over to Nick on her high-heeled sandals and kissed his cheek. "Love you. Bye. Bye, Faith."

Faith's response was lost as Britney raced out the door. Through the large windows, Nick watched his baby sister throw herself at the loser on the bike. Her boyfriend wrapped his arm around her waist, lifted her off the ground and kissed her.

A low growl rose in Nick's throat.

"I wouldn't if I were you," Faith said.

He blinked and realized she'd crossed the room and was flipping the Open sign on the door to Closed.

"If you can somehow sense I'm contemplating murder, I'll deny it," he said.

She turned the lock. "Actually, I figured you wanted to punch the guy. Or maybe cut off that straggly ponytail. I have to admit, I get that urge every time I see him."

"Get your scissors. I'll hold him down."

"Too late," she said, as Michael shot away from the curb, Britney on the back of the bike, her arms wrapped around his skinny waist, her cheek pressed against his back.

Nick took a step forward, ready to chase the bike like some crazed dog. "Did you see that? She's not even wearing a helmet. I've told her time and time again she has to wear a helmet." He tapped his fist against his thigh. "On second thought, forget your scissors," Nick murmured, imagining yanking motorcycle boy off his bike by his hair.

"It's not Michael's fault that Britney doesn't wear a helmet. Or that she's with him at all. She's an adult. She makes her own choices."

"He's unemployed, has questionable hygiene and a police record. He's trouble."

"Yes, he is. And hopefully Britney will figure that out before she gets in too deep. But again, no one is forcing her to be with him."

For the first time that day, Nick allowed himself to really look at Faith. Then wished he hadn't, when he noticed the way her soft pink top clung to her curves. "Speaking from experience?" he asked, more harshly than he'd intended.

She walked over to the desk and sorted through the bottles of nail polish on display, organizing them by color. "I've known my fair share of Michaels in my life. The bad boy has appeal but it doesn't last."

Appeal? Nick grabbed the chair and sat back down. He'd never understand why smart women fell for guys who weren't any good for them. "I hope Britney realizes that soon."

Picking up a pen, he tapped it against the desk as he tried to figure out if an invoice dated three months ago had been paid.

"You shouldn't do that," Faith said.

He stopped tapping. "Sorry. Bad habit."

"Not that. You shouldn't be doing Britney's work for her. She needs to learn to deal with her own problems. And she won't if you keep riding to her rescue."

"I'm doing her a favor." He matched up the amount on the invoice with a check listed in the register, marked the invoice paid and put it in the To Be Filed pile. "Not saving her from a runaway train."

"Look, I like Britney," Faith said, almost as if the fact surprised her, "but you're not helping her by doing everything for her. Or by rushing over every time she or one of your other sisters calls with a new problem they need you to solve."

Dropping the pen, he leaned back and studied her. "You don't have any family, do you?"

Her lips thinned. "You mean do I have anyone who can fix all my mistakes for me?" She shook her head. "I handle my own problems, thanks just the same."

"No, I mean do you have anyone you can count on?" he asked quietly, sensing her issues with him helping his family had more to do with her own reluctance to accept help. "Someone who'll be there for you when things get bad?"

"All I'm saying is that maybe Britney would accept more responsibility if she actually had to face the consequences of her actions."

He pinched the bridge of his nose. "You don't get it. Britney—all of my sisters and my mom, too—turn to me when they have a problem. Just as I turn to them when I need help. You think I'm some sort of pushover—"

"I didn't say—"

"But the truth is," he continued, standing up, "in my family, we're there for each other. That's what families do. That's what *I* do."

For a long moment Faith stared at him, as if he'd said they eat their young in his family. "You really are one of the good guys, aren't you?"

She didn't have to sound so damned surprised, did she? "Since I have no idea how to answer a question like that, why don't I just say that I haven't seen Austin since I got here. Is he hiding out back?"

Her brows drew together. "Trevor invited him to go swimming at the public pool. Since Kathleen is done at work before I am, she offered to take him home until I can pick him up."

"Well, you'd better get going then. I'm sure you don't want to be late."

She seemed taken aback. "I guess I should. Get going, that is. I'll see you around." She made it sound like a question.

"We have practice tomorrow. So unless you make Austin jump out of the car at the road, while it's still going, you'll probably see me."

"Right." Brushing her bangs out of her eyes, she crossed her arms. Then uncrossed them. Cleared her throat. "I'm supposed to work the concession stand during the first game. The tall blonde, the pretty one, is going to show me the ropes."

"Tracy?"

Faith nodded. Nick guessed Tracy was pretty enough, and she'd come a long way since she'd been called string bean in high school. But tall and thin had never been his type. He cast a surreptitious, and appreciative, glance over Faith's curves.

Maybe he could learn to like tall and thin.

"Are you and Tracy…dating?" Faith asked.

"What?"

Faith shifted, then straightened her shoulders. "She made a few comments about you that made me think…"

"Made you think we were together?" That was weird. He'd known Tracy practically forever and she'd never been the type to tell tales before.

"More like she was interested in you two being together. She's interested in you," Faith clarified.

His neck warmed and he rubbed the back of it. "Even if I was interested in Tracy—which I'm not—she was married to my cousin, so anything between us would be awkward as hell." Why Nick felt the need to clarify, he couldn't say for sure.

Something that could have been relief crossed Faith's face. "Oh, well. I guess she doesn't agree." Faith nibbled on her thumbnail, then dropped her hand in disgust when she realized what she was doing. "If you're not seeing her—or anyone else—maybe you'd like to do something Saturday night."

Her words came out in such a rush, Nick wasn't sure he heard her correctly. "What did you say?"

"Never mind." Her voice sounded strangled. "Forget it."

He rounded the desk and caught her before she made it through the back door. "I don't want to forget it. What I want is for you to say it again."

Her pretty mouth turned down, but for the second time she shocked the hell out of him. "I asked if you wanted to go out Saturday night."

Please say yes. Please, please say yes.

FAITH ATTEMPTED to swallow but felt as if she had a peach pit stuck in her throat. She'd had no idea this would be so hard. How did guys get up the nerve to ask a woman out, to face possible rejection? Honestly, she had a whole new appreciation for the men who braved this.

When Nick had taken hold of her elbow, she'd automatically latched on to his arm for balance, but now she couldn't let go. Under her fingers she could feel his tension. He stared down at her, his dark eyes intent. He was trying to read her. To figure out what she was up to.

That made two of them. After her talk with Tracy at the field the other day, Faith knew she needed to pick up her game. Or give up her plans of getting Nick to be her unsuspecting savior. Besides, she'd hated the idea of Nick being with Tracy.

Okay, that last part was probably her regressing back to the woman she used to be when she'd viewed every female as competition. It had nothing to do with the queasy feeling in her stomach when she thought of Nick taking Tracy and her daughter out for pizza. Or him kissing Tracy good-night on her front porch.

"You want to go out," he said, letting go of her and stepping back. "On a date. With me."

She nodded, then felt light-headed and realized she

was holding her breath. She exhaled. "We could go to dinner or—"

"What's going on, Faith?"

"What do you mean?"

"Last week you were upset to think people would see us together at the pizza place. You obviously don't trust me with your son. And now, all of a sudden, you want to go out? Do we have to leave the state to make it happen?"

"Don't be ridiculous," she said, forcing lightness into her voice. She should've figured he'd question her. Question her motives.

Which was probably a smart thing, considering her intentions were anything but honorable. Or honest. He enjoyed playing rescuer. So be it. She'd give him someone to rescue.

She needed to get him to care for her and Austin. Enough that he'd be willing to do whatever it took to keep them safe. "I enjoyed our dinner together the other night and I thought you did, too. Besides, I thought it'd be nice to get out. Take a break from being just a mom for an evening."

She stepped into the back room and he followed her. "So you want what, adult conversation? Why me? Why not Britney? Or another friend?"

Faith picked up a clean towel from the laundry basket and folded it. What could she say? That she didn't have friends? That she'd closed herself off as much as Austin had to keep from being hurt? To stop the regret and pain of leaving someone she'd come to care about?

"If you don't want to go," she said churlishly, "just say so."

"I didn't say that. But I am curious as to your motives."

"I asked because I like you," she exclaimed, throwing the towel on the shelf.

"Two weeks ago you didn't like me."

"I changed my mind," she mumbled. "And I...I thought you were attracted to me."

His eyes narrowed. "What are you looking for?"

"I don't know." The other day, when Tracy had made her interest in Nick clear, Faith had felt...possessive. Which was crazy. Nick didn't belong to her. But damn it, he'd kissed her.

She might not deserve it, but she couldn't pretend she didn't want someone like him in her life. Just once. Even if it wasn't real.

Before she could change her mind, she took two steps, closing the distance between them. Placing her palms on his chest, she felt the rapid beat of his heart. It gave her confidence to realize she could still make a man's heart race.

That she could make *this* man's heart race. This strong, honorable man.

No matter how much she wanted him to take control, to make the next move, he remained still as stone.

She forced herself to speak the truth—even though admitting this was harder for her than any of the lies she'd ever had to tell. "I can't stop thinking about you."

She wanted to, though. She didn't want this...this attraction to him. This pull. But it was there and she would use it to her advantage.

He bracketed her wrists with his hands but didn't push her away. "Didn't I already tell you not to play with me?" he told her fiercely.

She shivered at the strength of his rough fingers. Had she thought him nice? Safe?

"I'm not playing," she told him in a whisper, unsure at that moment which of them she was lying to.

Then she kissed him.

CHAPTER NINE

NICK'S MOUTH REMAINED hard and unyielding. For a moment. Then he yanked her against him, leaning back against the salon's dryer, and took over the kiss. Hot and slow, he simply glided his tongue against her lips. He tasted sweet, like the chocolate she'd seen him sneak from Britney's hidden stash in the desk drawer. And when his big hands went to her rear and pulled her even closer, so that she was nestled against his hips, Faith melted.

She slid her hands up his chest, over the buttons on his uniform and the shiny badge that declared him to be one of the good guys, until her fingers dived into the soft strands of hair at his nape. The stubble of his beard scratched her cheeks, the sensation a delicious contrast against the softness of his lips. He was warm and solid, and for the first time in way too long, she felt safe. For the first time ever, she felt like Faith Lewis, the woman she wanted to be.

Panicking, she tightened her grip on him. This wasn't real. It couldn't be. Not for her.

But she had to make him believe it was.

Rising to her toes, she pressed even harder against him, her breasts crushed against his chest.

He broke the kiss and moved her away. He was breathing heavily as he shoved a hand through his hair, his confusion and frustration evident. Almost as evident as the bulge behind his zipper.

He wanted her. The knot in her chest loosened and Faith shut her eyes against the rush of relief.

"Saturday night," he growled. "I'll pick you up at seven."

Then he walked out, his strides long, his back stiff. As if he couldn't wait to get away from her. The door slammed and she flinched before slumping against the dryer to try to catch her breath.

She rubbed a hand over her pounding heart. It had worked. She'd gotten what she'd wanted.

God help her now.

NICK WIPED THE BACK OF his hand against his mouth as he dashed out into the warm evening air, but he couldn't wipe away the taste of Faith. The feel of her.

He stalked down the street toward the station, where he'd left his car, hoping the short walk would help him get rid of his arousal. And his anger. She was messing with him and yet he still hadn't been able to resist her. Now, suddenly, she wanted to spend time with him? Ignoring the startled stares of an elderly couple, he crossed a street against the light.

Who would've guessed that underneath that timid, nervous exterior was a woman who excelled at playing up to a man? He'd thought that after she'd offered herself to him like some damn virgin at his altar last week, she'd back off. That she'd scurry back to being timid, mousy Faith Lewis.

He'd been wrong.

But he wasn't wrong about it being an act. Not all of it, he thought with a frown, as he slowed, nodding at a young mother and her toddler son. Nick didn't think Faith had been pretending with that kiss, or when she'd admitted she'd been thinking about him. That she liked him. The way she'd touched him, kissed him, had held elements of truth. But not the whole truth.

He clicked the button on his keys to unlock his car door. Once inside, he leaned his head back. She obviously wanted something from him and it wasn't dinner. Or at least, not just dinner. And it sure as hell wasn't sex, even if that kiss had suggested sex wasn't out of the realm of possibility.

He wouldn't deny he wanted to sleep with her. But more than that, or at least as much as that, he wanted the truth. Wanted her to come to him for help with whatever demons she was fighting.

Sitting up, he eyed the police station thoughtfully. Since Faith didn't trust him with her secrets, maybe it was time he figured them out on his own.

"UH...ARE THESE ALL THE clothes you have?" Britney asked early Saturday evening as she stared into Faith's closet.

Sitting in front of the cherry antique vanity she'd

stripped and refinished, Faith applied blush before glancing in the mirror to Britney. "Of course." Although she had to admit, the one thing she did miss about her old life were the shopping sprees. "Or did you think I'd stashed half my wardrobe under the bed?"

"I was hoping," Britney mumbled. She gave up on the meager contents in the closet and crossed to the large pile of clothing she'd carried in and dumped on the bed when she'd arrived, announcing she wanted to help Faith get ready for her date with Nick. "Luckily, Andrea's your size. And unlike Marie, she isn't stingy with her clothes. Wait until you see what I brought…here it is. What do you think? Isn't it perfect for you?"

Faith tipped her head to the side and studied the simple coral, sleeveless dress. "It's lovely. But I…I wouldn't feel right wearing it."

"Why not?"

"It's…too short."

Britney held the dress up to herself. The hem almost reached her knees. "It's a brave new century. Women can show their ankles and everything."

But Faith didn't want to wear the dress. It was bad enough she hadn't been able to convince Britney she wanted to get ready on her own. Now her boss wanted her to borrow her sister's clothes? *Nick's* sister's clothes? Faith had spent the past two nights tossing and turning thanks to her secrets and lies. Trying to get close to Nick for all the wrong reasons. She didn't need Britney and her sisters adding to her stress by being so generous and kind, as if she was one of their friends—and not someone they shouldn't trust.

"But I don't even know where we're going," Faith said.

"Which is why you should wear this. It's not too dressy. Not too casual. And look at the back." She flipped it around to show Faith the wide, crisscross straps. "These give it a hint of va-va-voom. Like I said, perfect."

Faith set her blush brush down. "I don't want va-va-voom. Tonight's just…a friendly dinner. Nothing more."

At least she hoped it would be friendly. From Nick's expression when he broke their kiss two days ago, "friendly" was the last thing on his mind. Throttling her was probably the first.

"Try it on," Britney urged, flipping the dress into Faith's lap before heading back to the closet. "Ooh… these are perfect for it," she said, holding out a pair of silver strappy sandals.

Faith sighed. The dress was soft and cool in her hands and those sandals really would look fantastic with it…. "Okay. I'll try it on."

She stood and, since Austin was downstairs using an hour of video-game time, shut the door before getting undressed. A few moments later, she studied herself in the mirror. The dress clung to her, showing off her ample breasts, and the bright color enhanced the light tan she'd acquired over the past few weeks watching baseball practices. Britney had been right about the shoes, too. For the first time in years, Faith looked and felt…pretty.

Sexy.

Ignoring her horror, she smoothed the skirt of the dress and twisted for a side view. It wasn't as if she was turning back into the person she'd been. She had too much respect for herself now, too much pride. Too much to lose. But, God, she resembled that woman.

But that didn't mean she had to act like her. There had to be a way for her to look like this and still be Faith Lewis.

"Wow, you are hot," Britney said from where she was sprawled on her stomach on Faith's bed. "And way too good for Nicky."

Faith lifted a hand to her hair. "Are you sure it's not too light?" After the salon's last appointment earlier, Britney had added more honey highlights to Faith's hair, then trimmed and styled it.

"I wish you would've let me add more." Britney swung around to sit cross-legged. "The blond warms your skin tone."

That was why she'd spent the past few years as a brunette.

"I've always wanted to go blond," Britney said, wiggling her eyebrows, "just to see if it's true they have more fun."

"You wouldn't really go lighter, would you?" Faith asked as she squeezed lavender scented lotion into her hand and rubbed it on her bare legs. "You don't have the coloring to pull it off."

Britney scrunched up her face. "Yeah, you're right." Grinning widely, she stood and picked up Faith's jewelry box before settling on the bed again. "But it would almost be worth it to see the looks on my brother's and sisters' faces. Oh," she said, digging into the front pocket of her jeans and pulling out her cell phone, "I'm vibrating."

As Britney took her call, Faith rubbed lotion onto her arms.

"That was Gene," Britney said, referring to the salesman who handled their account with the local beauty product supplier. "Good news—we'll be getting our supplies from J. H. Thompson on Tuesday."

"That's great." After Britney had failed to pay, the company had threatened to cease any further deliveries, and they were starting to run low on shampoo for color-treated hair.

Britney dug through Faith's jewelry, holding up a silver heart on a delicate chain before wrinkling her nose and putting it back. "Yeah, Nicky talked to Gene and worked everything out." She handed Faith a pair of silver earrings with three teardrop links hooked together. "Here, try these."

Inserting an earring, Faith looked at Britney in the mirror. "But I thought you were going to talk to Gene?"

She shrugged. "I was. But we were so swamped yesterday, and after you left, I took a walk-in customer. Nicky took care of it for me…." Her cell phone vibrated again, making a faint buzzing sound. Glancing at it, she bounced to her knees. "It's Michael! Hi, baby," she crooned into the phone as she fell onto her side.

Shaking her head, Faith twisted to get a better view of herself in the mirror. In her experience, people were treated a certain way because they acted a certain way. And since Britney acted helpless, people around her were more than happy to jump in and give her a hand whenever she needed one. Faith hoped someday the younger woman matured enough to handle things on her own instead of relying on her brother to take care of her.

Instead of trying to get Nick to rescue her, as Faith was doing.

She broke out in a cold sweat. That was *not* what she was doing. She didn't need a man to take care of her. Hadn't she taken care of both herself and Austin these past few years? And done a damn fine job of it, too, thank you very much. This…thing tonight with Nick was different from when she'd been on the prowl for a wealthy man.

The woman she'd been before might look similar to the woman staring back at her from the mirror, but she'd left that person behind the moment she and Austin had walked out of their town house in New York. Since then she'd had many different personas, disguises and names.

When she'd transformed herself into Janice Capshaw, she'd chopped off her hair, colored it red and wore contact lenses that changed her eyes from misty green to bright blue. Working as a bank teller, she'd told everyone she was a recent widow who'd moved to Cincinnati to be closer to her husband's family. For Ellen Jensen, she'd become a frumpy, brown-eyed, never-married single mother, had moved to Serenity Springs and started doing hair again. She'd ditched the colored contact lenses and continued to let her hair grow out when she'd moved to New Hampshire and became Lisa Risk, the black-haired wife of a marine stationed overseas.

Staring at her latest reincarnation, she felt her throat
burn. She didn't know who she was anymore. But she
knew one thing for certain. She'd never be Lynne
Addison again.

AT SEVEN O'CLOCK, Nick rapped his knuckles against
Faith's door. The thump of a ball being dribbled mingled
with laughter and shouting as a group of kids played
basketball a few houses down the road. He searched for
Austin among them but didn't see him.

The kid had come a long way since that night at Nero's
when he'd refused to play video games with Trevor and
his friends. During the last few practices Nick had seen
him joking with the other kids, and Austin and Trevor had
hung out a few times, as well. But there was still something…off about Austin. Something that told Nick
whatever Faith was hiding affected her young son, too.

And Nick no longer doubted Faith was hiding something. His instincts, plus her surprise dinner invitation
followed by that shocker of a kiss, confirmed it for him.

A salt-scented breeze off the ocean ruffled his hair
as he knocked on the door again, this time harder. Hell,
he'd been so fired up after leaving the salon the other
day he'd headed straight for his desk at the police
station. But as he sat at his computer, ready to dig into
Faith's past, he'd realized he was letting his personal
feelings—and, okay, his ego—get in the way of his
better sense. He needed to keep things in perspective,
take a step back and treat this thing with Faith as he
would any other case he had to solve.

No more getting personal.

The door opened and Nick turned.

Aw, shit.

His heart beat frenetically as he skimmed his gaze over Faith. Her dress was the color of a summer sunset, with a plunging neckline. The swinging hemline ended at midthigh. A pair of sandals added several inches to her height. She wore bright peach polish on her toes. She'd done something to her eyes, too, making the green seem darker. Sexier.

"What the hell did you do to your hair?" he asked.

She flinched, but recovered quickly, even as her hand brushed the flutter of long bangs to the side. "Britney gave me a trim."

"It's different," he said grudgingly. "Lighter."

"She added a few highlights."

He tugged on his earlobe. Here he'd been planning to subtly interrogate her over dinner, in a safe environment, all the while keeping his emotional and physical distance from her. And she ended up looking like some damned blonde bombshell straight out of a fantasy.

So much for that brilliant idea.

"You're beautiful."

She plucked at the fabric of her skirt and cleared her throat. "Thank you. But I can't take any credit. Britney played stylist. I think she felt it was like having a life-size Barbie doll. With more realistic measurements."

His fingers twitched to find out if her hair was as soft as it looked, her skin as smooth. He stuck his hands in his pockets and tried not to think about her measurements. "Ready to go?"

"Let me get my purse."

A minute later, they made their way down her front walk to his car. Their arms brushed and the hair on his stood on end. After opening the car door for Faith, Nick took his time walking around the back of the car to the driver's side. He needed to get a grip. Just because the way she looked, the way she made him feel, threw him for a loop didn't mean anything had changed.

"I hope Italian's okay," he said, sliding into the car and starting the engine. He pulled away from the curb. "I made reservations at Borgo Romano's."

"I've never heard of it."

"It's about twenty miles inland." He glanced at her. "You seemed so upset that people saw us together at Nero's, I figured you'd be more comfortable away from Kingsville."

"That—that's really—" if she said nice, he'd kick her out on her lovely ass "—sweet of you."

He clenched the wheel, grinding his teeth. *Sweet?* That was even worse. "I had selfish motives," he said. "I didn't want to have to worry about you being nervous the entire evening. Though I sort of thought we were past that."

"We were. We *are*." She shifted and he felt her hesitation before she laid her hand on his leg. He wanted to jump out of his skin, but managed to keep still. "And I have to admit," she said, her voice shaking slightly, "I'm glad we'll be out of town and away from people who know you. It'll be...nice...not to have to share you with anyone else tonight."

He gently squeezed her hand, then set it back in her lap before gripping the wheel again. Did she think that just because she'd toned down the sex-kitten act, he wouldn't recognize it for what it was? Why couldn't she be straight with him? Whatever she needed his help with must be big for her to put on an act that obviously made her uncomfortable.

For the remainder of the drive, Nick worked to set Faith at ease. They discussed the baseball team and especially Austin's joy at being named starting pitcher. Faith told Nick how she and everyone else in the salon had teared up when a mother and three daughters came in and had their waist-length hair cut off so they could donate it to Locks of Love, an organization that provided wigs to ill children. By the time Nick held open the restaurant's door for Faith, she was smiling at his story about when he'd gone to talk to Mr. Kearns about Mrs. Farrell's complaint.

"At least he wasn't naked when he answered the door this time," Faith pointed out.

"Still, I could've lived without seeing him in his leopard print thong."

She laughed, and at the husky, uninhibited sound, his chest tightened. In a purely nonpersonal sort of way.

The hostess led them through the large, dark room to a corner table. Nick held out a chair for Faith before taking his seat across from her. A fat votive candle in a tall red holder shimmered with light in the center of the table. After a quick discussion on the merits of white sauce versus red, they ordered the pasta. A few minutes later their waitress, a chubby, bespectacled brunette with a bright smile, delivered their drinks.

He took a swallow of his beer. "So, what's Austin up to tonight?"

"Britney took him out for ice cream and to rent a movie. It was nice of her to give up her Saturday night to watch him."

"Brit loves kids," he said. "I'm sure she's happy to hang out with Austin."

Faith sipped her red wine and, setting her glass aside, cleared her throat before laying both hands in her lap. "Not as happy as he is. I think he has a bit of a crush on her. But please," she added hurriedly, "don't let him know I said that. He'd be mortified."

"He won't hear it from me. And I'm not surprised he's fallen for Brit. Males of all ages love her. By the time she was walking she already had me and my dad wrapped around her finger. Especially Dad."

The waitress delivered their appetizer—smoked mozzarella fondue with garlic-rubbed toasted crostinis—and a basket of warm braided bread sticks. She set down two small white plates and left again.

Nick gestured for Faith to go ahead, and she spooned some of the gooey cheese mixture onto her plate. "Britney doesn't talk very much about your dad."

Nick chose a bread stick and took a bite. "I doubt she remembers him. She was only four when he died."

Faith carefully spread some cheese onto a crostini before taking a nibble. "He had a heart attack?"

As it always did when he thought of that day, Nick's stomach knotted. "Yeah."

"He must've been awfully young."

"Thirty-nine." Nick stared at his glass, remembering how his father had loved nothing more than spending a rainy Sunday afternoon with a cold beer while watching his beloved Red Sox. "He used to brag about how he never got sick. It drove my mom nuts since she caught every cold or flu bug us kids brought into the house. He claimed he was so healthy he didn't need to get regular physicals. If he had…" Nick sat back and wiped a hand over his mouth.

"Do you think something could've been done to prevent his heart attack?"

"I've asked myself that a thousand times and to be honest, I'm not sure I want to know." He shrugged as if to rid himself of the remnants of grief that clung to his memory of his father. "We were supposed to go fishing that day. Just the two of us—no girls allowed, he'd said. He'd promised to wake me up early." Nick slowly straightened his fisted hands. Forced himself to take another bite of bread, to chew and swallow. "Instead, we all woke up to my mom screaming."

"That must have been awful for ya'll," Faith said softly.

He frowned. *Ya'll?* Seemed that story Faith had spun for him about her past wasn't entirely true. Unless people from mid-Pennsylvania spoke with Southern-tinged accents. Could be she'd picked up the dialect of one of the places she'd lived while traveling with her husband. But Nick doubted it.

"I can still hear Mom screaming. My sisters crying." He wouldn't press her about her slip. After all, any cop worth his salt gathered his evidence first before making his case. "I called emergency services even though I could tell by looking at him it was too late. The worst part was tearing my mother away from him so the EMTs could work on him."

That's when his mother had first turned to him, burying her head in his skinny shoulder, her body racked with sobs. When he'd realized he needed to step into his father's shoes and take care of his family.

"I'm so sorry." Faith squeezed his hand, the gesture somehow more honest than when she'd touched him in the car. "Your mom and sisters are lucky to have you."

"We're lucky to have one another." Now that he'd laid the groundwork by not only putting her at ease, but by opening up to her, he linked his fingers with hers. "What about you? Who do you go to when things get tough? When you need a shoulder to cry on?"

Sitting back, she freed her hand from his. She took a long drink of her wine and when she set the glass down again she laughed, but the sound was at odds with her shuttered expression. "I'm a single mother. I don't have time to lean on anyone else."

"Not even Austin?"

"Don't take this the wrong way," she said slowly, "but I don't think relying on my nine-year old son is a wise, or healthy, decision. For either of us."

Because he agreed with her, and because his own cir-cumstances were different from hers, Nick let her criticism of his upbringing go. Besides, he admired what a great mother she was to the boy.

"Do you ever wish you had more support around you? Family members? Close friends?"

"I'm used to being on my own," she said briskly, pushing her plate aside. She rested her forearms on the table, angling her body toward him—the better to showcase her breasts in that damned dress. "Besides, I have Austin and now Britney. And…well…a few weeks ago you said you wanted to be my friend…."

And he thought he could stay professional? Not likely. Not when she looked at him with such hope, as if she really did want his help. "I meant that."

This time her grin was less forced. "See? I have plenty of support."

He finished off his bread stick and helped himself to the cheese spread. If his hunch was right and she'd been a victim of abuse, she needed to learn to trust someone again. So he wouldn't push her for more than she was ready to give.

As their waitress delivered their salads and cleared away their used plates, Nick studied Faith. The candlelight flickered over her face, picking up the golden strands in her hair. Now that he'd had time to get used to her new appearance, he had to admit the hair, the makeup, the outfit—it all suited her.

"I almost ran a background check on you," he said when they were alone.

With a soft clang she dropped the fork she'd been using to nudge aside slices of black olive on her plate. "What?"

He bit into a cherry tomato, the flavor of it exploding in his mouth. "It would be easy enough to do. I have the skills and the clearance to find out pretty much anything I wanted about you."

She pushed her chair back as if ready to bolt, her face white, her eyes huge. "Did…did you?"

"No. And I won't. For one thing, it'd be unethical to use my position that way to appease my curiosity."

"You considered it," she said, leaving no doubt that made him almost as guilty as if he'd committed the sin. But at least she relaxed her death grip on the tablecloth.

"I did. And the only reason I'm telling you any of this is because I…" He stabbed a piece of lettuce. "I'm interested in you. Interested in getting to know the real you and not some persona you've adopted."

She blushed. "I don't know what—"

"Or some story you've concocted. Like," he continued casually, "the one where you grew up in Pennsylvania even though every once in a while I detect a trace of Southern in your voice."

Her jaw dropped. "I…that's… I don't—"

"You have my word I won't go behind your back. I won't even ask you any questions about your past if you promise not to lie to me anymore."

He didn't think she'd agree. Hell, he wouldn't be surprised if she tossed her wine at him. Instead, she searched his face.

Finally, she nodded and scooted her chair closer to the table. "I promise."

At least she didn't try to claim she'd been telling him the truth all along. That had to be progress.

"It's not as if I have anything to hide," she assured him in a rush. "I just… I've made some mistakes and I…don't like to dwell on the past."

"No one's perfect, Faith." Nick reached across the table, palm up. After a brief hesitation, she placed her hand in his. And that one tiny gesture meant more to him than he could say. "I want to be a part of your life," he told her, surprised by how right it felt to admit the pull she had over him. "So whenever you're ready to stop running from your problems, you let me know. I'll be here."

CHAPTER TEN

FAITH GOT OUT OF HER CAR and stared through the dark lenses of her sunglasses up at Andrea Frey's imposing colonial-style brick home. The midday sun beat down, and the air was heavy and humid. But that wasn't why Faith's lightweight top clung to her skin. It wasn't what made sweat bead on the nape of her neck and roll down her back. She was nervous.

She snorted, then raised her eyebrows in an innocent expression when Austin shot her a quizzical glance from across the hood. But soon he went back to what he'd been doing all morning—sighing loudly, rolling his eyes and vibrating with impatience.

"Come *on*, Mom," he said. "Let's go."

"I'm coming. I'm coming," she muttered, and wondered when on earth the two of them had switched bodies. She usually had to prod him to hurry along. "Here, you carry this…" She handed him her large tote bag. "And I'll get the cake."

Picking up the plastic cake carrier from the backseat floor, she straightened, used her hip to shut the door, and looked up at the house again. There was a line of cars on the long driveway, so she'd chosen to park on the side of the quiet road. That much easier to leave if she needed to cut out early.

Her palms grew damp. Had she thought she was nervous? More like sick-to-her-stomach petrified. But she couldn't back out, not when she'd promised Britney she and Austin would attend the Coletti family's annual Fourth of July picnic. Not when Austin was so excited about spending the day with Trevor.

His new best friend, plus swimming in a private, in-ground pool, all the food he could eat *and* fireworks and a campfire after the sun set? Her boy was in heaven.

She, on the other hand, was heading straight to hell. Because as much as she wanted to make her son happy, he wasn't the main reason she'd agreed to come here. It was a way to get closer to Nick. Besides, it wouldn't hurt to integrate herself into the town. Into people's lives. Wasn't that what people did when they started over?

Befriending the Colettis—one of the most well-liked and respected families in town—helped make it seem as if she belonged in Kingsville. A means to an end.

Guilt pricked her conscience but she shook it off as she followed Austin up the curving stone pathway to the house. She wasn't doing anything wrong. Not really. And she wasn't out to hurt anyone—that had to count for something.

Her pulse picked up speed when she noticed Nick's car at the end of the driveway. Checking her reflection in its window, she shifted the cake so she could fix her bangs. Okay, so maybe there was some anticipation mixed in with her anxiety. Which was crazy. She had no business wanting Nick or, God forbid, enjoying his company. But she did.

Forcing herself away from the car, she followed Austin up the winding path that led to the front porch. After their dinner date, Nick had walked her to her door and brushed his lips against hers in a sweet good-night kiss. The next day, he'd sent flowers. Not a bouquet but a pot of bright red zinnias. She'd smiled the entire time she'd planted them in her little garden. And when she'd called to thank him, she'd spontaneously invited him over to join them for dinner, since she'd made her mama's special fried chicken. Later in the week, he and Austin had spent an hour after baseball practice trying to teach her how to bat. Then they'd all gone out for ice cream.

Things were going well. And while letting Nick get close was a big mistake—it was somehow going to backfire on her—she couldn't seem to stay away.

A loud shriek made her jump. Trevor, wearing only a pair of bright blue swim trunks and carrying a squirt gun the size of a small bazooka, ran barefoot through the thick grass of the front yard. He zipped between her and Austin, forcing Faith to skid to a halt.

"Hi," Trevor said. He was amazingly dry for someone obviously in the midst of a squirt-gun battle. "Can I carry anything for you, Ms. Lewis?"

"No fair hiding behind neutral parties," a deep voice said from her left.

A deep, familiar voice that made her shiver in awareness. She turned as Nick reached them, and that awareness blossomed into sharp, aching need. His mussed hair was damp, his cargo shorts and dark T-shirt wet with several water spots. He held a gun identical to Trevor's on his broad shoulder, making him look boyish and sexy.

"When Aunt Marie yelled at you for squirting her you said everything was fair in war," Trevor told him gleefully.

"If that's true," Nick mused, scratching his stubble-covered cheek, "then I guess I can do this."

In one swift move, Nick tossed his gun aside, feinted right, then caught a giggling Trevor as he darted in front of Faith. Nick lifted Trevor onto his shoulder so that the boy's legs dangled across Nick's back. Holding him with one arm, Nick tickled his ribs until he howled with laughter.

"Give?" Nick asked, patting Trevor's back.

"Ne-never," Trevor gasped, trying to lift his squirt gun.

Nick shook his head and tickled him again. "Boy, you are as stubborn as your mother. Maybe I should—"

A steady stream of water in his face cut him off. They all turned toward Austin, who held Nick's abandoned gun. Pride surged through Faith. He'd come so far from the sullen kid he'd been less than a month ago.

Nick shook his head. "Two against one, huh?"

"Yeah, Austin!" Trevor cried. "Get him again!"

Except this time when Austin squeezed the trigger, Nick twisted so that Trevor took the brunt of it. Yelping as the water soaked his hair, he lifted his own gun and retaliated. Nick quickly set his nephew on his feet and jumped out of the line of fire, behind Faith.

"Why don't you two plan a sneak attack on Uncle Steve?" he suggested over her shoulder.

Trevor's face lit up. "Great idea. Come on, Austin, let's reload."

Whispering about offensive maneuvers, they ran off.

"I hadn't thought you were the kind of guy to throw a family member to the wolves like that," Faith said.

"It's the boys you should be worried about." Nick wiped the water off his face with his sleeve. His shirt rose, revealing several inches of tanned, toned stomach. "Steve keeps the hose with him at the grill for just these situations."

Wondering what it would be like to touch him there, above the waistband of his low-slung shorts, Faith's fingers twitched. She sure could use one of those coastal breezes about now.

She forced her eyes up to meet his and shifted the cake in her hands. "Maybe you should stick close to the hose, as well. Looks as if you lost the war," she said, inclining her head to indicate his wet shirt.

"Not the war. Just the battle." But then his smile faded as his dark gaze drifted over her, the heat of it pricking her skin. He reached out and, as light as that summer breeze she'd been wishing for, traced the tip of his finger over the thin strap of her halter top at her shoulder. "Pretty," he murmured. "Like the sunrise."

She couldn't move. Could barely breathe. "I…uh… saw it, in the window at Jayne's downtown…"

It was eye-catchingly bright, subtly sexy and a far cry from how she usually dressed. When she'd tried it on she hadn't just felt pretty, more importantly, she felt…comfortable. She felt like herself.

And that had scared the crap out of her because she couldn't afford to get comfortable. To be herself. Not when she might have to become someone new again.

Still, she'd had to have the outfit. A muscle jumped in Nick's jaw as he slid his finger across her shoulder and down her arm to her elbow, trailing gooseflesh in his wake. Stepping back, he pulled a pair of sunglasses out of his front pocket and put them on.

"Let me get that for you," he said gruffly, taking the cake from her.

"Oh. Thank you." Except without it she had no idea what to do with her hands. So she wiped them down the sides of her white walking shorts. Crossed her arms and then let them hang at her sides before picking up her bag from where Austin had dropped it.

"Everyone's out back," he said. Then he took her hand.

She almost stumbled. She'd come to learn he was big on touching. He'd pressed his palm to the small of her back when they left the restaurant. Wrapped his arms around her, his solid chest against her back, as he went through the motions of the proper batting swing. Brushed his fingertips against her cheek as he tucked a strand of hair behind her ear while she ate her ice-cream cone.

It was…sweet. She couldn't remember a time when a man had wanted nothing more than the simple pleasure of touching her. And realizing how much she enjoyed it, enjoyed being with him, was all too frightening.

So instead of focusing on how it felt, his rough, large palm against hers, she took in their surroundings. The Freys' house was a mix of brick and wood, with double front doors, tall, gleaming windows and immaculate landscaping. There were trees, shrubs and flowers to soften the austere lines of the house and make it warm and welcoming, and as far as she could tell, there wasn't one blade of crabgrass in the lush lawn.

It was a far cry from her own weed-choked backyard and spotty windows.

They rounded the garage and were met by the low hum of voices mixed with music. "This is a lovely house," Faith said, withdrawing her hand from his before anyone could see them.

"Andrea and Steve are happy here."

She slowed her steps as the voices grew louder. Many, many voices from the sound of it. "I especially liked that first flower bed, the one with the miniature roses. Does Andrea garden?"

He laughed. "Andrea doesn't do dirt. Or anything related to getting dirty. Luckily, her in-laws enjoy it, so they handle the gardens for her."

As they reached the backyard, Faith's throat was so dry, not even the enticing scents of grilling meat could work moisture into her mouth. One look at the crowd talking and laughing on the long patio made her step back, bumping into Nick's solid frame.

He steadied her with a hand to her upper arm. "Everything okay?" he asked.

She edged away from him—and the backyard—

hugging her arms around herself. *Okay?* Let's see…she was spending the day with a nice family. Her son had a new best friend and was acting like a normal nine-year-old again, and she had the interest of the sexiest man in town.

Everything was awful.

She was a liar. Worse, even she was beginning to believe her lies. Beginning to hope that she could stay in this town, be a part of these people's lives and give her son the permanency he craved.

That she could be Faith Lewis forever.

Ever patient, Nick stood there, staring at her from behind his sunglasses, his posture relaxed, the damp hair at his nape curling. Forcing a smile, she looked up into his handsome face. "Everything's perfect."

IF THAT WAS TRUE, Nick thought, he'd borrow Mr. Kearns's thong and wear it on his head.

He led her back around the corner, giving them some privacy.

"I realize my family can be a bit—" High-pitched female laughter rose above the conversation and blaring rock music, and he winced. "Overwhelming, especially when we're all together."

"I'm way out of my element here," Faith admitted. "I've never even been to a family picnic before. My mom's idea of celebrating the Fourth was boiled hot dogs and sparklers."

"Staples of any decent party celebrating our nation's independence," he said lightly, more grateful than he wanted to admit that she was telling him this. "We've got both, so you're already ahead of the game."

She laughed softly, the sound shoving out of his head his good intentions not to push her. Leaning down, he paused long enough to catch her quick intake of breath, to feel her exhalation wash over his lips.

"Oops!" a cheery female voice called. "Sorry."

Faith jumped and Nick straightened to glare at his sister. Kathleen stood a few feet away, her dark, chin-length hair held away from her face by a pair of red sunglasses.

"Pretend I was never here," she said, walking past them with her hand up, blocking her face.

"I should go," Faith said, slipping past him. "I need to, uh…check on Austin and—" she snatched the container out of his hands "—deliver my cake."

"Guess she's not impressed by the old Coletti charm," Kathleen said as Faith hurried off. "Although why you'd attempt a make-out session here in front of God and your family is beyond me. Anyone could walk up and interrupt you."

Nick shut his eyes and tilted his head from side to side until his neck cracked. "It wasn't a… We weren't… Never mind."

"Don't go," Kathleen said, grabbing his arm and pulling him toward the driveway. "I was heading out back to see if someone could give me a hand with Dana. We went on an ice run and she fell asleep as soon as we left the store's parking lot."

Dana, Andrea's young daughter, adored her aunt Kathleen above anyone else. "You took her with you?"

"She was getting cranky and wouldn't settle down for a nap, and I needed to get out of the house before I mutinied and took over the kitchen."

At Kathleen's ancient SUV, Nick opened the back door and handed her the small cooler he found on the floor, before unbuckling a sleeping Dana from her car seat. "I take it Andrea is Captain Bligh?"

"Who else? You know how she gets...."

"Neurotic and anal?" He lifted Dana out of her seat. Her head lolled forward, her long, dark lashes fanned against her chubby, pink-tinged cheeks.

Kathleen shut the door for him while he raised Dana so her head rested on his shoulder. "She actually complained about how I arranged the pepperoni on the antipasto tray. When she showed me a picture from a magazine of how she wanted it done, I knew I had to get away from her before I did something I'd regret."

"That's probably for the best. We wouldn't want a repeat of Christmas 2002."

"Hey, now, she started that."

Nick grunted. He had learned early on not to get in the middle of his sisters' arguments. But from what he could recall, Andrea *had* started the conflict by being her critical self most of the day. By the time dinner rolled around and she'd commented that the gravy Kathleen made had enough lumps to qualify as ham-flavored pudding, Kathleen had had enough.

Though dumping the bowl of mashed potatoes on Andrea's head may have been overkill.

"Let's go through the garage," Kathleen suggested when he started for the backyard. "It's so noisy out back and I'd hate for Dana to wake up."

He shifted the sweating toddler higher in his arms, felt a wet spot through his shirt of what had to be drool. "The only way this kid is waking up is if a marching band starts performing next to us. And even that's no guarantee. If you want to avoid Andrea, just say so."

"I want to avoid Andrea."

"Fair enough."

In the garage, they circled Andrea's shiny black Lexus. "Look how clean the interior of her car is," Kathleen muttered. "I'm telling you, that's not normal."

Nick stepped inside and waited in the cool hallway while Kathleen shut the door and set down the ice. Female voices drifted to them from the kitchen and he could pick out his mother's husky laugh. Thankfully, Andrea had insisted on having central air installed when they'd built this house. Holding Dana was like hugging a furnace. She murmured in her sleep, her puckered lips opening and closing. He gently brushed her sweat-dampened hair off her forehead. A seriously cute mini furnace.

"So, you and Faith, huh?" Kathleen asked over her shoulder as they climbed the stairs. "Your taste in women has improved since Nancy Janov."

Dana stirred and lifted her head. He rubbed her back as they walked through the airy and bright game room that opened to the foyer below, and she relaxed again. "There's nothing wrong with Nancy."

"She has a chipmunk voice."

"Good point." He walked past Kathleen into Dana's bedroom. Like the rest of Andrea's house, his niece's room looked as if it had been torn out of a decorating magazine. Hardwood floors, soft, moss-green walls he'd helped Steve paint, and white furniture all went together perfectly with the red-white-and-green bedding.

He carefully laid Dana on her back in the plush crib, marveling that she didn't stir, not even when he took off her tiny red sandals. Kathleen flipped on the baby monitor and, linking her arm through his, tugged him out of the room.

"All I meant was that I think it's great. The you and Faith thing. I like her, and Austin's terrific."

"Yeah, he is. But the thing with Faith and I, it's not… We're not…" He raked a hand through his hair. "Hell. I'm not sure what it is."

"You've really got it bad, don't you?" Kathleen asked with a laugh.

Shoving his hands into his pockets, he walked to the railing above the foyer. He took off his sunglasses and hooked them in the collar of his shirt. While he loved all of his sisters equally, he and Kathleen, the two oldest siblings, had always been especially close. He couldn't think of anyone whose opinion he trusted more. "What would you do if you suspected someone you were… starting to care about…was hiding something from you? Something from their past."

She shrugged. "If it's in the past, why worry about

it? I'd sure hate for someone to hold some of my mistakes against me."

"It's not about holding anything against anyone," he said in frustration. "It's about helping them deal with whatever happened so they can move on."

So Faith could learn to trust again. Starting with him.

"Hmm…well, I guess if I really cared about this person," Kathleen said, "I'd make it clear I was there for them no matter what, and when they were ready to share with me whatever happened, I'd be waiting."

"I already did that," he grumbled.

"Let me get this straight. You think Faith has some deep, dark secret—"

"I didn't put it that way."

"—so you did the right thing by giving her space, but now you're upset because she's not working within your timeline?" His sister shook her head, her expression bemused. "Don't be such a bonehead."

So much for seeking her advice. "I want to help her. Is that so wrong?"

"No, it's not wrong. But you can't force someone to open up to you. If you're right and something did happen to Faith, maybe it's too painful for her to talk about. To anyone."

"*If* something happened, if she's running from something, she needs to deal with it, not pretend it never happened."

"You don't get to decide that." Kathleen patted his hand as if to take away the sting. "Just as you can't save someone who doesn't want to be saved."

"MY MOM LIKES YOU."

At Britney's words, Faith bobbled the white porcelain bowl she'd just dried. She carefully set it on the counter with the rest of the clean dishes that hadn't fit into the dishwasher. She'd hoped helping with kitchen duty would give her a short reprieve from the Coletti family's warm acceptance of her and Austin. Everyone had gone out of their way to make them feel welcome. As if they truly wanted them there.

It made her feel like crap.

"What did she… I mean, how do you know?" Faith asked.

Shrugging, Britney drained the water from the sink and dried her hands on a towel. "I can tell. And she wouldn't have told you the secret to her famous potato salad if she didn't." Britney wiggled her eyebrows. "I think she's hoping you and Nick stay together."

Faith's stomach dropped. "But we're not together."

"You went out last weekend," Britney said, "and then you had him over for dinner. Plus, you're the first woman he's ever brought to a family picnic. In my book, that's together."

"Nick didn't even invite us," Faith said. "You did."

"Yeah, but he asked me to."

Faith's mind spun and she grabbed on to the counter. "What?"

"I would've asked you anyway," Britney said, "but before I could, he suggested it."

"Why would he do that?"

"He told me it was because he's scheduled to work

this evening and he didn't want to invite you, only to have to leave. I think he was afraid you'd turn him down," she said with a smirk.

"No," Faith murmured. "I don't think that's it."

Although if he had been the one to ask, she probably would have refused. Attending a family get-together with her boss was different from going as the guest of the man she'd been on a date with.

He'd had Britney invite her because he didn't want Faith to feel uncomfortable, especially since he'd have to leave for work. And he probably suspected her plans to celebrate the holiday would be staying at home with Austin and cooking on her portable grill. Plus, he'd kept his promise of not pushing her.

How was she supposed to keep resisting a man like that?

Lauren, Ethan's pretty, petite blonde wife, came in carrying her screaming two-year-old daughter, Julie, on one hip and wide-eyed, nine-month-old Michelle on the other.

"What did you do to my little jewel?" Britney asked, taking the toddler from her mother. Julie wrapped her arms around Britney's neck and pressed her face into her shoulder. Sobs shook her tiny body.

Lauren hitched Michelle higher on her hip. "Your goddaughter needs a time-out," she said, frazzled. "She took Dana's doll and when Dana tried to get it back, Julie pushed her."

Britney rubbed Julie's back and made shushing sounds. "I'm sure she didn't mean it."

Oblivious to the turmoil around her, Michelle grinned at Faith, showing off her two top teeth. Faith couldn't help but smile back.

"Mean it or not," Lauren said, "I'm going to take her up to the game room and sit with her until she calms down."

Britney waved a hand. "You go and enjoy the picnic. I'll take her."

Britney and Julie walked out and a minute later, Faith heard the unmistakable sound of a child's high-pitched giggle.

She glanced at Lauren, who had emitted a low growl. "Everything all right?" Faith asked.

"The last time Britney handled one of Julie's time-outs, Brit gave her a piece of gum to get over the trauma of sitting in one place for ten whole minutes. It took me two hours to get all the gum out of Julie's hair."

Faith pressed her lips together to keep from laughing. "That's terrible."

Lauren's own lips quirked and she shook her head. "Okay, so it's sort of funny. But I don't want to go through it again. Hey, listen, would you mind watching Michelle for a few minutes?"

"What?" Faith tucked her hands behind her back. "Oh, I don't—"

"She'll be fine. Michelle's not the least bit shy. See? She already wants you." The baby held her arms toward Faith, babbling incoherently. "Please. I need to get upstairs to supervise those two. It'll only be a few minutes."

What else could she do? Especially after the baby practically threw herself at Faith. Lauren rushed out of the room.

Though she hadn't held a baby in close to eight years, it all came back to her. Faith pulled the bottom of Michelle's red gingham sundress down to cover her diaper, then couldn't resist rubbing her cheek against her soft flaxen curls.

"You're a doll, aren't you?" she asked, and Michelle babbled some more.

Then she patted Faith's face with her chubby hand. "Mum-mum."

Faith laughed. "Not quite. And you'd better not let your mommy hear you calling other women that or you'll hurt her feelings."

"Lauren's used to it," Nick said from behind her. Faith jumped and whirled around. Michelle giggled and batted her shoulder. "Michelle calls everyone mum-mum. Even her daddy."

Faith forced herself to relax. To return Nick's smile. She hadn't been alone with him since that humiliating moment when Kathleen had interrupted them earlier. Though she'd tried not to, she'd found herself searching for him several times as she'd visited with his family and close friends. Found herself wanting to be with him.

Nick carried two plates loaded from Andrea's designated dessert table. "I thought I'd better bring you some before it's gone. Besides, you've been in here for thirty minutes. You must've worked up an appetite."

Instead of being panicked at the idea of him watching her so carefully, she was actually…flattered.

"You keeping an eye on me?" she asked, flirtatiously. All part of her act, she told herself.

"Always," he said with a wink. He looked around. "Where's Brit?"

"She's upstairs with Julie and Lauren."

"Good. Then I can eat her dessert."

Trevor and Austin raced into the kitchen from the hallway. They were both wearing swim trunks now and had towels around their necks.

"Mom," Austin said, "can me and Trevor go swimming?"

"May Trevor and I go swimming," she corrected automatically.

He sent Trevor a moms-are-so-lame look. "Yeah. That's what I meant. So, can I?"

"I don't know," she hedged. "It's been a few years since you took swimming lessons—"

"You let me go swimming at the public pool at the park," he said.

"That's different. They have trained lifeguards."

"Aunt Marie is getting in with Dana," Trevor said. "And my uncle Steve and Ethan are going to watch us from the deck. Uncle Steve's a doctor and Ethan can do CPR and stuff."

She bit her lower lip. Steve was a doctor, but she wasn't sure how much a dermatologist knew about saving a drowning victim. Still, there were plenty of people milling around if the boys got into trouble. And

Austin had been at the swimming pool with Trevor almost daily for the past two weeks. When she'd picked him up last week, she'd seen his improved skills when he swam the length of the pool for her.

She nibbled on her thumbnail. "I suppose it's all right...."

"Thanks, Mom!"

They were out the door and racing across the yard before she could remind them not to dive into the shallow end or run on the pool deck.

"Do you want to go out?" Nick asked. "There are plenty of places to sit and watch."

Through the family room picture window Faith could just make out Austin's head as he and Trevor reached the pool. Ethan said something to Trevor, making the boy laugh. Then Ethan scooped him up and tossed him into the water. Her shoulders stiffened when Austin got tossed in next. She only relaxed when she spied both boys laughing as they climbed out the other side.

"No," Faith said, loosening her hold on Michelle when the baby began to squirm. "He'll be fine."

No one here was going to hurt him. Her boy was safe.

"Come on," Nick said, gesturing to the family room. "Let's sit."

Not waiting to see if she followed, he walked over to the plush love seat in front of the window. By the time Faith reached him, he'd set the plates on a glass-topped coffee table and taken forks and napkins from his back pocket.

She stopped at the end of the love seat and realized

that from this vantage point she had a clear view of the pool. And her son.

"I wasn't sure what you liked," Nick said as he took a squirming Michelle onto his own knee. "So I brought some of everything."

Then he smiled at Faith. Before she could rationalize her feelings or what she was about to do next, she leaned down and kissed him.

CHAPTER ELEVEN

NICK'S BREATH BACKED UP in his lungs as Faith's lips clung to his for a heartbeat. Then two. The muted sounds of the ongoing celebration outside filtered into his sister's living room. Wrapping his arm around the baby, he cupped the back of Faith's head with his free hand, his fingers delving into her hair.

Michelle squealed and hit Faith's cheek with her chubby fists. Laughing softly, Faith leaned back. "Looks like someone's jealous."

He loosened his hold on her, sliding his palm over her bare shoulder and down her arm. "I'm popular with the toddler set."

Michelle bounced in an effort to get his attention, and he lifted her so she stood on his legs. He tore his gaze from Faith long enough to kiss the baby's smooth cheek. "You're still my number one girl," he told Michelle.

Seemingly satisfied with that, she babbled some more, then did a few deep knee bends, her hands wrapped around his fingers for support.

"Should I ask what that was for?" he said to Faith as

she sat down close enough to him for their knees to touch. "Or just be grateful and keep my mouth shut?"

Not that he wasn't grateful. But other than that kiss she'd laid on him at the salon, she rarely initiated any type of physical contact between them. This kiss had been different. More…real.

"Maybe it was a thank-you because you brought me cake."

"Don't forget the brownie," he reminded her. "And I wrestled that last piece of my mom's blueberry pie away from Ethan."

"Sounds dangerous."

"It was touch and go for a moment."

"But you prevailed. My hero." Then she kissed his cheek, laughing when Michelle pushed her away.

"Next time I'll bring you the whole damn pie," he promised solemnly.

Faith's smile dimmed. "It wasn't just for the food— although I would've been very disappointed if I'd missed out on blueberry pie. It was for…everything. For suggesting we sit here so I have a clear view of Austin in the pool, instead of making me feel overprotective because I'm nervous about him swimming. For asking your sister to invite—"

"Brit has a big mouth," Nick grumbled, feeling like a child. "I would've asked you myself, but I thought you might feel too awkward."

"You were right. I'm not sure I would've come if you'd asked instead of Britney. You're always doing stuff like that, making things easier for me. Being considerate and kind and caring." Instead of sounding as if she appreciated those things, though, her tone indicated that they somehow pissed her off. "You shared your family with me and my son, you taught me how to hit a ball past the pitcher's hill—"

"Pitcher's mound."

"You like babies and kids and they all seem to adore you right back. You're great with Austin and you keep your promises." She picked at the spotless love seat, her voice barely above a whisper when she asked, "How could I not want to kiss you?"

His pulse was pounding in his ears, and he didn't know if he should laugh, be insulted at her obvious displeasure or apologize. "How about we stick with me being grateful?"

Lifting her head, she exhaled with a laugh. "That's probably the best choice."

Michelle reached for the plate of desserts. "You're not the only one who's glad I brought these." Setting her back on his knee, he scooped up red velvet cake with a plastic spoon and fed it to her before taking a larger bite himself. He grunted in appreciation.

"Did you make this?" he asked.

Picking up the plate he'd brought her, Faith nodded. "Mi— Uh, my ex didn't like it, so I haven't made it in a long time. I hope it's not too dry...."

He took another bite before giving Michelle more. "Even better than Andrea's." Leaning forward, he lowered his voice. "And if you tell her I said that, I'll deny it."

"She won't hear it from me."

Scraping frosting off Michelle's chin with the side of the spoon, he winked at Faith. "I knew I could trust you."

Why that made her blanch and duck her head, he wasn't sure. But the hair at the nape of his neck stood on end. She was still holding something back.

After glancing out the window—presumably to check on Austin—Faith set her plate on her lap and started in on the pie. Michelle squealed, holding her arms out and opening and closing her chubby hands. Faith gave her some of the filling and the baby grimaced comically, her lips puckering even as she continued to smack her lips.

Nick laughed and nuzzled her neck until she giggled. "You'd better stick with the cake there, kiddo."

"She's adorable," Faith said, smoothing back Michelle's fuzzy, flaxen hair. "When I was pregnant, I'd hoped I was having a girl. Someone I could dress in frilly clothes, do her hair and show her off."

"Like a living doll?" Nick asked, setting a squirming Michelle down. She crawled over to a large basket of magazines and began tossing them out one by one.

"I guess so. But then everything changed." Faith put her plate on the coffee table and stood, crossing to look out the window. "When I held Austin for the first time, I stopped wishing for that little girl. He was mine and that was all that mattered."

Nick ground his back teeth so he wouldn't spit out the questions burning on his tongue. He'd promised he wouldn't ask her anything about her past, and damn it, he'd keep his word. Even if it killed him not to know why her reflective tone had an underlying sadness, instead of joy, as she recalled her son's birth.

He picked up Michelle who, now that the basket was almost empty, had plopped down on her diapered butt to rip those magazines apart, and joined Faith at the window.

"Good form," Nick commented, when Austin did a cannonball into the pool. "Although if you want to see a big splash, wait until Ethan gets in. It's like a tsunami."

They stood in companionable silence watching Austin and Trevor try to outsplash each other.

"Thank you," Faith said softly. He glanced at her but she continued to stare outside. "Thank you for sharing your family. I've never had this..." She gestured outside. "For the most part it's just been me and Austin. I've never been able to count on anyone else."

Hitching Michelle to one side, he wrapped an arm around Faith's waist. She tensed momentarily, but then relaxed against him, laying her head against his shoulder.

"You can count on me," he vowed. And that was a promise he meant to keep.

TWO DAYS LATER, Nick carried a case of soda in each hand as he walked up the steps and into the dusty converted trailer the baseball teams used as a concession stand. The sunlight filtering in through the open door, even combined with a shop light overhead, did little to break up the gloomy shadows inside.

"Did you get it yet?" Nick asked as he set the soda down. He wiped the back of his hand across his forehead.

"Almost," Austin said, grunting as he tried to move

the heavy plywood that covered the opening where people could order their snacks or drinks. Even standing on a step stool, he was a few inches too short.

"Here," Nick said, coming up behind him. "Let me give you a hand." He reached around Austin and swung the plywood up. "Can you latch it?"

Nodding, Austin leaned onto the ledge, stretched up and placed the heavy metal hook into the metal ring.

Nick let go and backed up. "Great. Now why don't we—"

"Austin?"

"Sounds like your mom's looking for you," Nick said, sliding the step stool under the counter next to the commercial-size cooler. "You'd better let her know where you're at."

"Austin!" Faith called again, her tone frantic.

Glancing outside, Nick spotted her racing past the Port-A-Potties, her voice rising as she shouted her son's name again.

"I'm right here," Austin said from the doorway.

"In the concession stand," Nick added, when she whirled toward them. Nick crouched and set a bottle of grape flavored sports drink in the cooler.

Bursting inside, Faith blanched as she stared at her shirtless son. "Oh, my God," she breathed, her voice unsteady, a book clutched to her chest. "What happened?" Grabbing Austin's arm, she shoved him behind her. "What did you do to him?" she demanded of Nick.

In the process of reaching for another bottle, he froze. "Do to him?"

"I'm helping Nick," Austin said quickly, brushing past Faith to stand between them. "We're just putting stuff away in here."

"You need a kid to help you?" Her suspicious tone irritated Nick until he saw real fear in her eyes. "Don't you think it's inappropriate to be alone in here with a half-naked child?"

Nick rose and shut the cooler door. "What are you accusing me of, Faith?" he asked softly.

"Mom, we're just helping Coach, that's all," Austin said, his voice strangled with humiliation.

Wild-eyed, she glanced at her son. "We?"

"Me and Trevor and Trevor's mom. She's the one who brought the drinks, and since we were early for practice she asked if we could put them away."

"Kathleen left not three minutes ago," Nick said, realizing he still held the bottle when his grip dented the hard plastic. He set it on top of an unopened case of soda. "Trevor went with her because he left his batting gloves in the car. I'm surprised you didn't see them."

Faith blinked. "I didn't. I—"

"Other than those three minutes," Nick continued, in the same calm tone he used when trying to diffuse a potentially volatile situation on the job, "I haven't been alone with your son. If you want that confirmed, I can give you Kathleen's cell phone number."

"But…his shirt…"

"Trevor and I took them off," Austin said, pulling their shirts from the metal table where the boxes of candy would be set up for sale. "It's, like, a bajillion degrees in here."

More like ninety, but given that Nick's own shirt clung to him and the hair at his neck was damp with sweat, he could appreciate Austin's estimate.

"The Whites and Gage are here," Trevor said, sticking his head and bare shoulders in the doorway.

"Why don't you two go on out with them and start warming up?" Nick said. "I'll be there as soon as I've finished."

"Don't forget," Trevor said, as he took his shirt from Austin and pulled it over his head, "you promised we could have sliding practice today."

Nick set the dented bottle aside and ripped open the case of soda. "How can I forget when you guys have reminded me about a dozen times already?"

Trevor ducked out again, but Faith stopped Austin before he could follow suit. "Next time you're going to leave the field area, ask me first. Do you understand me?"

"But you weren't here—"

"Then you'll have to wait until I get back," she said firmly.

"Fine," he mumbled, and then bolted.

Opening the cooler door, Nick began setting cans of soda on the middle shelf. Faith cleared her throat. "I...I owe you another apology."

"Nope."

He sensed, more than saw, her surprise. "But—"

"You were protecting your son. And I shouldn't have asked Austin to help me without getting your permission first."

After a moment of stunned silence, Faith asked, "Did you just admit you were wrong?"

He shoved the next can onto the shelf with enough force to tip it over. From the disbelief in her voice, you'd think he was some sort of egotistical asshole. "It's unusual—the being wrong part," he said drily, straightening the can, "but chances were it was bound to happen at least once in my life."

"I still overreacted. The book I'd been waiting for came in at the library—" she held up the paperback "—and Austin was in such a hurry to get here, I dropped him off. But when I came back and couldn't find him…"

Nick stood and closed the cooler door. "Like I said, it was my fault."

The sight of her looking so uncertain and remorseful made him want to take her in his arms and console her. To promise her he'd never hurt her or Austin. To pretend she hadn't acted as if he'd done something unspeakable to her son.

Turning away, he concentrated on breaking down the cardboard soda container. "We were both wrong," he said, more gruffly than he'd intended. He tucked the flattened box in the recycling bin and pulled the plywood sash shut. "I'd better get out there. The rest of the kids will be here any minute."

She blocked his exit. Lifting a hand as if to touch him, she dropped it back to her side when he stepped back. "Nick, please, I—"

He shook his head. "Not now. We can talk about it

later but…" He stabbed a hand through his hair and exhaled heavily. "Just not now."

She pulled her shoulders back, and for a moment he didn't think she'd give him the time he needed to process everything that had just happened. And what it all meant. He needed that time. And that distance from her.

Luckily, she only swallowed and then walked away.

Nick crossed to the door but couldn't make himself step out into the bright sunlight. Not yet. He pulled it shut and turned off the light, enclosing the trailer in darkness. Pressure built inside his chest, his breathing grew rapid, his hands curled into fists. With a low growl he spun and punched the side of the cooler. Pain shot up his arm, but the only thing that stopped him from pummeling the thing was the awareness that if he broke his hand, he couldn't work.

Gulping in the stale air, he tipped his head back. The anger that had simmered in his gut since he'd realized what Faith thought he'd done quickly grew into a toxic brew of fury and disgust. Disgust at himself for being so focused on her all this time, for being so certain she'd been the one who'd suffered abuse, that he hadn't considered Austin might have been the victim. Fury at the sick son of a bitch who'd preyed on that sweet kid. But worse was the sense of helplessness. Someone had hurt Austin.

And there wasn't a damn thing Nick could do about it, except make sure it never happened again.

FAITH'S STEPS SLOWED as she approached Nick's bungalow. His neighborhood was quiet, the tidy street lined with older, well-maintained homes. She placed a hand over her roiling stomach. After she'd left him in the concession stand, she'd hid in her car for the entire practice. Even now her face heated as she remembered the way she'd treated him. How she'd jumped to conclusions.

Stopping on the sidewalk in front of his place, she chewed on her thumbnail. His car was in the driveway and light flickered through the large window to the right of the front door. She wiped her damp palms down the sides of her jeans and, after a quick prayer for courage, walked up and…turned around and went back down the stairs.

Oh, God, she couldn't do this. She couldn't even take a full breath. Dizziness threatened to overwhelm her. Bending at the waist, she wrapped her arms around herself and concentrated on breathing. In through the nose. Out through the mouth. Until the feeling returned to her hands and feet.

Before she could change her mind, she hurried back up to the porch and knocked on the door. The muted sounds of a television set drifted through the open window and a moment later, the door opened.

Nick frowned. "Faith. Is everything okay?"

She opened her mouth, readying some frivolous lie about being in the neighborhood. Or maybe she could pretend she'd just been lonely and wanted his company. He would accept that, accept her at face value. Because he cared about her. And the last thing she wanted was to lay herself bare to him, to see the warmth in his eyes turn to disgust when he found out how she'd failed as a mother.

"Yes. No. I mean, I'm fine." She stopped babbling and swallowed down her nausea. "I'm sorry I didn't call first, but I was hoping I could talk to you?"

He studied her in that intense way of his that used to make her cringe. But this time, instead of trying to hide behind a cool stare, she let him see her unease. Her worry that he would slam the door in her face. That once he found out the truth, he wouldn't want her anymore. Finally, he stood aside.

"Thank you." She walked into his large living room, which opened into a dining area. The room itself was a study in brown. Beige walls and carpet, long taupe curtains and a dirt-colored leather couch that had seen better days. The only color came from the baseball game playing on the large flat-screen television on the wall.

"Can I get you something?" Nick asked as he snatched a newspaper off one of the tan armchairs before gesturing for her to sit. "Have you eaten?"

It was then that she noticed a bottle of beer and a plate with the remains of a T-bone steak and baked potato on the wooden coffee table. "I didn't mean to interrupt your dinner."

"No problem. I was done." He looked around as if trying to decide what to do with the papers in his hand before shoving them on top of his baseball hat on the matching chair. "I can make coffee or I have soda."

At this point she was one short step away from over-loading. The last thing she needed was caffeine. "A glass of water would be great," she said as she perched on the edge of the chair.

He grabbed the plate and walked into the kitchen and around a corner. A short minute later he came back and handed her a glass of water. The ice clinked in her shaking hands.

Sitting at the end of the sofa, he took a long drink before setting his beer back down. "I didn't hear you pull in. Where'd you park?"

"I walked."

"It's almost three miles from your house."

"I used the time to think." She'd needed to figure out what to say. After a quick sip of water, she set the glass on the table. "Kathleen took the boys to the drive-in."

"Yeah, they told me about it before practice."

Faith twisted her fingers together in her lap. "So you know how excited Austin is. He's never been to a drive-in before."

"Seemed to me he was more exciting about spending the night at Trevor's house afterward."

"It's his first friend sleepover," she blurted. "The first time he's spent the night away from me since…since I left my husband."

"You okay with him being away from home? Away from you?"

"I…" No, she wouldn't lie to him. Not tonight. "Even though I trust Kathleen and even though I'm sure he'll be fine, I'm still terrified something will happen to him."

Admitting the truth was much harder and much easier than she'd expected.

"What are you doing here, Faith?"

"I want it to be real," she whispered.

"You want what to be real?"

She cleared her throat, noticing for the first time that his feet were bare. "I want my life to be real. I don't want to keep pretending. Or lying. Especially to you." Raising her head, she met his eyes. "You were right. I'm not from Pennsylvania. I grew up in South Carolina, outside of Charleston."

"Why lie about it?"

"I was embarrassed." And with that admission, guilt threatened to swamp her. "We lived in a rented trailer on this small weed-choked lot. God, I hated it. I always thought I was so much better than that…" She pressed her lips together. "We had nothing. My mom tried but…" Faith shrugged and took another drink. A drop of water from the sweating glass fell on her bare leg and she used her wrist to wipe it away. "She had one dead-end job, one lousy relationship, after another."

"What about your father?"

"I was around Austin's age when I got up the nerve to ask her about him, but she wouldn't even tell me his name." Faith remembered the moment as if it had just happened. The latest in her mother's long line of lovers had recently taken off. Faith had been in front of the TV, wrapped in a quilt to beat the chill of the January wind blowing through the cracks around the windows, and her mother had been chain-smoking at the tiny kitchen table. "So I asked her to at least tell me why he left and…she just stared at me. She seemed so broken. Even as a kid I realized how beaten down she'd been by life. She told me they all leave."

"Some people have bad luck with relationships."

Faith smiled sadly. "She chose men who wouldn't stay. I decided I wasn't going to end up like her. That I was better than that," she said in self-disgust.

He tapped her knee. "You should be proud of everything you've accomplished."

"When I was younger, I wanted more than a career and the ability to pay my own way. I wanted it all. And I wanted it given to me. I dreamed of a wealthy man taking me away to live a life of luxury. By the time I was sixteen, I knew the chances of some Prince Charming riding up to my trailer and rescuing me were slim to none. So I decided to find the right man myself."

Elbows on his thighs, hands clasped between his knees, Nick studied her. "I take it the high school sweetheart you told me about was a lie, too."

Since he made it sound like a statement and not a question, she didn't bother answering. "The day after graduation, I moved to New York City. I attended cosmetology school full-time, working nights as a cocktail waitress at a private club in Manhattan. That's where I met my husband." Though he was fifteen years her senior, he'd been so charming. So confident and sophisticated. And a successful businessman, wealthy enough to make all of her dreams come true. "I tried to convince myself I was in love with him. But what I really loved was what he could do for me. The things he could buy me… That shocks you, doesn't it?" she murmured. "You with your happy, well-adjusted family."

"I'm not shocked. And just because I'm from a small town doesn't mean I don't realize some people prefer security over love. Hell, I'm not even saying you were wrong." Sitting forward at the edge of the cushion, he tucked her hair behind her ear. "But I am sorry you settled for so much less than you deserved."

A lump formed in her throat and she jumped to her feet, bumping the table. Water splashed over the side of her glass. "I got what I wanted. We had a whirlwind romance, the kind I'd always dreamed of. He took me to fine restaurants, bought me jewelry and clothes. It was so easy to pretend that girl from the trailer had never even existed."

She began to pace. "I got pregnant on purpose," she continued impassively, as if she was speaking about someone else. "I needed a way to hold on to him, and it worked." The worst part was, she couldn't even regret it. Not when her devious act had given her Austin. "As soon as I became his wife, I thought I had everything I wanted." Pressing her forehead against the window, she stared out at the burst of sunset. "I didn't even care about the baby," she whispered. "What I really wanted was to keep my new life."

Tears clouded her vision. She tensed as Nick set his hands on her shoulders. "Anyone who's ever seen you with Austin can tell how much you love that boy."

"I do love him. More than anything," she said fiercely. She crossed her arms. "The first time I held him, it was like…I finally knew what love was. He's all that matters. He's the reason for everything I've done since I had him." Though Nick's house was warm, a chill gripped her, made her shiver. "He's the reason I left my husband."

Nick nodded, his expression grim. "Because he hurt Austin."

Hearing it out loud was like a slap across the face. Other than Allison Martin, an attorney who'd helped them when they left New York, Faith had never told anyone the truth. But Nick cared about Austin. Cared about both of them. She needed to trust Nick. She wanted to trust him.

"Yes." She managed to push the word out past the tightness in her throat. "He did hurt him. He molested him."

CHAPTER TWELVE

"GOD, FAITH," Nick said, raking an unsteady hand through his hair. "His own father?"

He wished he was back at the concession stand so he could punch the cooler again. Better yet, he wanted to find Austin's father so he could take his frustrations out on the sick bastard.

"I didn't know," she whispered bleakly. "For so long I had no idea what was going on…" She pressed her quivering lips together. "He was hurting my baby and I was totally clueless."

Nick took hold of her elbow and led her to the sofa, then sat next to her. "It wasn't your fault."

"How can it not be? I should've realized something wasn't right. Austin had always been a good-natured kid. But it got so he'd blow up when I asked him to put away his toys or shut off the TV. And he was having a difficult time in preschool. Shoving and biting the other kids. Putting him to bed was a nightmare. I thought it was a stage." She wiped her palms up and down her thighs, rocking with the motion. "Until one night when I came home early from a meeting and walked in on my husband exposing himself to our son."

Bile rose in Nick's throat, but he was sure it was nothing compared to how Faith must've felt when she'd witnessed the abuse firsthand. "Was he brought up on charges?"

Nick was filled with trepidation when she hesitated. This wasn't some suspect he was interrogating, after all. This was Faith. And though it wasn't easy for her, she was finally telling him the truth.

"Yes," she said. "After the trial, Austin and I left New York and never looked back. I just… After what happened at the concession stand, I had to explain why I reacted the way I did."

He took her hands in his. "You were protecting your son. You shouldn't have to apologize for that. Ever."

"Thank you." She squeezed his fingers. "I can't tell you how much it means to have you understand."

While he couldn't fault her for her actions, there were still some things that weren't clear. "Why all the lies about your past?"

Averting her gaze, she shrugged and withdrew her hands. "At first, it was easier to make something up in an effort to avoid people asking me questions that I didn't want to answer. But it was also…is also…a great way for me to pretend none of it ever happened. A way for Austin and me to have a true new start. That's all I've ever wanted."

He grimaced. "Guess I didn't make that easy on you, huh?"

The sight of her small smile made his pulse jump. "I

can see where my evasiveness would cause some people to be even more curious. Besides, you've more than made it up to me."

"How so?"

"By showing me there are men out there who always keep their word," she said, pressing her hand to the side of his face. "By being the type of strong, honorable man I can trust with my son. And my secrets."

"What about your heart?" he asked hoarsely, his hands fisted at his sides to keep from reaching for her.

He heard her quick intake of breath. "You deserve better than me."

He'd meant it to be a gentle kiss, a kiss to show her she was more than good enough for him. That he cared for her and her son. But she ran her tongue over his lips, clawed at his shirt.

He eased back. "Faith, I don't—"

"Please. I want to forget everything, just for a little while."

Laying her back against the sofa's armrest, he followed her down, supporting his weight on an elbow as he kissed her ravenously. He hadn't realized how starved he was for her until this very second. Sliding his hand under the hem of her shirt, he brushed the silky skin of her stomach. She quivered and wrapped her leg around his, pulling him closer.

The sound of a car door slamming jerked him back to his senses. He leaned back and couldn't help feeling smug at the flush of arousal on her face. The way she had to blink several times before frowning up at him.

"What's the matter?" she asked.

"While I'm not expecting any more company to-night, we might want to continue this in the bedroom. That is, if you *want* to continue this."

Please, God, let her want to.

Stroking the hair at the nape of his neck, she nodded. "Lead the way."

Leaping to his feet, he grabbed her by the hand and pulled her up. Not letting go of her, he managed to shut the window, then lock the door, which he couldn't resist pressing her against for another long kiss. With his arms on either side of her head, he brushed his mouth across her cheek and down along her jawline.

"Where were we going?" he asked, before nipping at the rapid pulse at the base of her throat.

She gasped and bucked against him. "Uh…the, uh, bedroom?"

"Right." He sucked gently, and felt her moan vibrate her throat. "Then again, this is a nice spot, too."

Her head fell back and he placed openmouthed kisses up the side of her neck, pausing behind her ear to inhale the subtle floral fragrance she wore. "You were worried about privacy," she reminded him, clutching his biceps.

He raised his head. "Privacy's good. So's a bed."

"I'm all for both," she said, using her short nails to lightly trace circle designs over his arm muscles, then his wrists.

At the thought of her doing that to other parts of him, of having her hands on him, their bodies together skin to skin, he clasped her hand and tugged her to his bedroom. By the time he flipped on the light, she was breathless and laughing.

"Sorry," he said with a grin as he backed her toward the bed. "Too fast for you?"

She shook her head. "I'm flattered."

Too bad now that the heat of the moment had passed—so to speak—she didn't look flattered. As a matter of fact, she looked…apprehensive. Which made perfect sense. He doubted she'd been with anyone since her divorce. And the thought of him being her first, after all this time, was both humbling and exciting as hell.

"I think we can afford to slow down some," he said, forcing himself to do just that. He cupped the back of her head and gently kneaded the tension out of her neck. With a soft sigh, she shut her eyes. "I've been thinking of this for too long to rush through it," he admitted.

Her eyes popped open. "You've thought about us…like this?"

"This is one of the variations." He edged closer until their thighs met. "A tamer one, actually. Turns out I have a very vivid imagination when it comes to you."

She blushed. "I'm afraid my fantasies about us have all been fairly tame."

And just like that, Nick went from aroused to painfully hard. Wrapping his free arm around her waist, he drew her against him, massaging not just her neck but her lower back right above her tailbone. "Why don't we try out one of my ideas first? If either one of us still has enough energy to move when we're done, we'll give one of yours a shot."

FAITH LOCKED HER KNEES so she didn't melt in a puddle right then and there, simply from his husky words and the images they invoked. Unable to speak, she moved her head. It must've passed for a nod because he kissed her warmly before stepping back.

Taking the bottom of her shirt in both hands, he lifted it an inch, then stopped. "May I?" he asked, his eyes dark with desire.

She'd meant what she said—that she wasn't worthy of him. Hell, she was still lying to him. But tonight, she'd do what she could to show him what he meant to her.

She lifted her arms. Nick peeled the shirt up, inch by torturous inch. His knuckles grazed the indentation at her waist, the slight bumps of her rib cage and the sides of her satin bra before caressing her inner arms. Once the shirt was off, he tossed it onto a large dresser, where it slid across the glossy surface and landed against the attached mirror.

She stood transfixed by the hungry look on his face, the stiffness of his jaw as he skimmed his fingers over the swell of her breast. Her nipples tightened, straining against the fabric of her cream-colored bra.

"Will you take your hair down for me?" he asked.

Tugging the band off, she shook her head and combed her fingers through her locks so they settled across her shoulders. Then, before she could change her mind, she reached behind her back and undid her bra. It slithered down her arms to the floor between them.

He made a sound not unlike that of someone being punched in the stomach. "None of my fantasies even came close to this," he admitted reverently. "You're beautiful."

During her life, she'd had countless men tell her that. Some meant it, some said it because it was expected. But for the first time, she believed it. She felt beautiful. Before she had time to revel in the feeling, to enjoy the thought of being intimate with someone she truly cared for and respected, Nick closed the distance between them. Wrapping one strong arm around her waist, he bent, took one nipple into his mouth and sucked.

Her head lolling back, she gripped his shoulders.

He released her breast and kissed his way to the other one, his stubble causing an erotic friction against her delicate skin. "Let go," he whispered. "I've got you."

Nick brushed his lips up and down the slope of her breast. Her fingers dug into the solid muscles of his shoulders. "I…I can't."

"You can," he said, looking up at her. "I won't let you fall."

Then he ran his tongue around her areola, causing the beaded tip to tighten further. She forced her arms down to her sides, her fingers curling into her palms. When he took her in his mouth again, she went boneless. He rubbed a work-roughened palm over her other breast until she panted and writhed against him.

He lifted his head and yanked her against him. A wave of dizziness rushed over her, intensifying when he took her mouth in another searing kiss. Breaking the kiss, he let go of her long enough to strip his shirt off.

Her heart fluttered. He was all toned, golden skin, his chest covered in dark hair, his abs nicely defined.

He reached for her again, and when she shook her head, he froze. Faith could tell, from the muscle jumping in his jaw, the way his chest rose and fell with each rapid breath, and of course, the telltale bulge behind his zipper, that he wanted her.

Not the girl who'd grown up with all the wrong dreams, or the woman who'd made so many mistakes, who'd married for all the wrong reasons. Not the woman who'd lied, cheated and stole to keep her son safe. Nick, the most honorable, honest person she'd ever known wanted *her*. Faith Lewis.

Tears stung her eyes but she blinked them back before he could see. Lightly combing her fingers through the wiry curls on his chest, she smiled. "This is better than any of my fantasies."

After tracing circular patterns over his shoulders and across his pecs, she went lower, down to his belly button, then to his sides. Still using her nails, she stroked the faint line of hair that ran from his navel into the waistband of his low-slung jeans. He inhaled sharply, creating a small gap between skin and denim, and she took advantage of it by dipping her fingers inside.

"Maybe I should rethink my idea of going first," Nick growled. "After all, ladies first."

"Why don't we forget the fantasy stuff?" She kissed him, withdrawing her hand. "This is one case where I think reality may give fantasy a run for its money."

Then she scratched her nails over his erection

through his jeans. He jerked even as he pressed himself into her hand. Before she could do more than cup her palm around him, he lifted her off her feet. She squealed as she fell back onto the bed. Nick followed her down, his hard body pressing her into the mattress as he kissed her deeply.

His hands skimmed over her, down to her shorts. He made quick work of undoing the button and sliding down the zipper. She lifted her hips as he knelt beside her and yanked off both her shorts and her panties and tossed them aside. Her skin heated as his intense, dark gaze took her in.

"Did I mention you're beautiful?" he asked, his voice rough.

All she could do was nod. She couldn't worry about her stretch marks or those extra ten pounds on her hips. Or the fact that she hadn't been with a man in more years than she cared to think about. All she could focus on was Nick. On the anticipation building within her over what he would do next. On what she wanted to do to him.

Luckily, she didn't have to wait long. Starting at her hipbone, he smoothed his hand down her thigh, over her knee to her ankle. But instead of making a return trip as she'd hoped, he caressed the top of her foot. She squirmed.

"Ticklish?" he asked, giving her other foot the same treatment.

"No, it's just…I don't think anyone's ever touched my feet before."

His grin was hot and wicked. "Sweetheart, I'm going to touch you everywhere."

His tone, along with the knowledge that Nick always kept his word, made her pelvis contract and moisture pool between her thighs. Gliding his hand up her leg, he leaned down and kissed her. Caressing her chest, her arms, even gently massaging her wrists and fingers. Her bones seemed to liquefy under his rough palms as he kneaded away the tension in her shoulders. As much as she wanted to touch him, to explore his body as he was exploring hers, it took all she had to muster enough strength to simply hold on to him.

But then his touch—and his kiss—changed. Both became more demanding as he stroked her rib cage and her stomach. Nudging her legs apart, he skimmed his knuckles up the sensitive skin of her inner thighs. Her tension began to build again, spiking when he flicked his thumb over her aching center. She whimpered into his mouth and lifted her hips, almost coming off the bed when he slipped one thick finger inside her.

Raising his head, he sat up. Faith dropped her hands to the mattress, curling them into the bedspread as he slowly worked her with his finger. His free hand went to her breast where he lightly pinched her nipple. Sweat beaded on her skin. She panted. Nick added a second finger, stretching her so completely, so wonderfully, she was surprised she didn't burst into a million splintered pieces.

Instead, she kept climbing higher. "Please," she

gasped as he twisted his fingers inside her, creating the most delicious feeling. "Please, Nick."

He stroked his thumb over her. Once. Twice. At the third touch, her climax ripped through her, scattering her thoughts, suffusing her with pleasure.

Her body tingling, her mind a hazy cloud, she pried open her eyes to find Nick watching her. A soft laugh burst out of her. "You're looking awfully smug," she said.

He raised his eyebrows. "Do I have reason to?"

"Oh, definitely." She pushed herself onto her elbows and gave him a lingering kiss. "And now it's my turn."

"Your turn to be smug?"

"My turn to touch you. Everywhere."

NICK'S BLOOD ROARED in his ears. "I'm not sure that's the best idea," he rasped—although his body would disagree.

Faith tipped her head so that her hair slid over her shoulder like a golden cloud. "Why not?"

He tried to swallow, but his mouth was too dry. Still supporting herself on her elbows, she was like some fantasy come to life with her milky skin flushed from her orgasm, her mouth red and glistening from his kisses. "I'm not sure how much I can handle," he admitted, not giving a damn if she knew how much power she had over him. How much he cared for her. "I want you too much and I…I don't want to lose control."

She smiled slowly and sensually. Sitting up, she kissed him again, nipping his lower lip. He groaned and she eased back and met his eyes. "It's okay," she said, undoing the button of his jeans. For all of his good intentions, he didn't have the will to stop her, especially when she pressed her hand against his straining erection as she pulled his zipper down. "I trust you. I think…I think you're the first man I've ever trusted," she added in a rush.

Well, hell. How was he supposed to be all honorable and strong when she said something like that? When her soft hand dipped under the waistband of his briefs to brush against him?

Rolling off the bed, he pulled open the drawer of his nightstand and took out protection. With the condom between his teeth, he pushed off his pants and underwear, then tossed the condom onto the mattress as he climbed back on the bed. Faith got on her knees, wrapped her arms around him and pulled his head down for another mind-blowing kiss. The hard tips of her breasts rubbed against his chest and he pulled her against him. Lifted his hips so his arousal rode the incredibly soft skin of her lower stomach.

She ran her hands over his shoulders, down his arms and around his waist to his back. She kissed his jaw, his neck and then his upper chest while she did that incredible thing with her nails above his tailbone. His fingers squeezed the round globes of her rear as he thrust against her.

Her hands gripped his outer thighs, her mouth moving down his stomach. Lower. Lower until his lungs burned with his pent-up breath. "Faith," he moaned, grasping her hair, unsure if he wanted to lift her head or beg her to keep going.

She looked up at him from under her lashes and his

penis jumped. "It's just a kiss, Nick," she assured him, reminding him of when he'd said the same thing to her on her porch a few weeks ago.

Then she kissed him. His sigh turned into an almost soundless curse as she took the tip into her mouth and sucked. His head fell back, his fingers massaging her scalp. When she lightly scraped her nails up the length of him, he yanked her away before he exploded right then and there.

Gripping her behind her thighs, he pulled her legs out from underneath her and flipped her onto her back. Her laughter only served to inflame him as he ripped open the condom and covered himself. She was already reaching for him when he used his knee to nudge her legs apart and enter her.

He wanted to slow down, to take his time and show her what she meant to him. But she was so hot. So wet. And the surprise on her face, as if she'd never felt anything as good as what he was doing to her, was so raw, so honest, he couldn't help but pump into her again and again.

His arms shook with the effort to hold himself off, but he wanted to see her face, wanted to watch her every second they were together. She bent her knees and took him in even farther, her heels pressing into the mattress by his hips as she matched his frenetic pace. Their bodies grew slick with sweat, their breathing ragged.

Her hands slid to his shoulders, her nails digging into his skin. Sensing she was as close as he was, Nick reached between them. He'd no sooner rubbed his knuckle over her than she began to pant, her moans turning into whimpers as her orgasm coursed through her. She kept her eyes on his, let him see her pleasure as her body convulsed underneath his, contracted around him. Pushed him over the edge.

He gripped her hips and lifted her butt off the bed as he repeatedly thrust into her until his own climax broke over him. His arms gave out and he collapsed on top of her, gulping for air.

"I hope I'm not too heavy," he said when he could speak, "because I seem to have lost the ability to move."

"That's okay. I'm pretty sure I stopped breathing about ten minutes ago."

Nick stared down at Faith's beautiful face. They shared a smile and then she laid her hand on his cheek. They kissed, a soft, sweet meeting of lips that about had his already full heart bursting.

She pulled back and sighed. "If you keep that up, I'm not going to want to leave."

"You could stay." The thought of Faith in his bed, of being able to make love to her again in the middle of the night, of waking next to her in the morning, tempted him more than he cared to admit.

"I can't." But at least she sounded disappointed. "I asked Kathleen to have Austin call me between movies, and since I don't have a cell phone…"

"You need to get home," he said, rolling off of her and grabbing his clothes. "Give me three minutes to get dressed and I'll drive you."

She sat up, her hair a wild tangle, beard burn marring

the creamy skin of her neck and shoulders. He'd never seen anything so beautiful.

"Thanks," she said, getting to her feet. She pulled her panties on and picked up her bra.

"Don't thank me. I have an ulterior motive. I'm not ready to let you go yet." She looked so startled—and scared—he silently cursed himself. Keeping his expression clear, he added, "I was hoping I could run a few scenarios by you."

Hooking her bra behind her back, she frowned. "What kind of scenarios?"

He shrugged. "Just a few ideas I've had ever since the first time I kissed you."

"If any of them involve me dressing up like a cheerleader or wearing your handcuffs, I'm not interested."

"No costumes or accessories, I promise. But there is one that involves your salon chair and a bit of spinning."

Her lips pursed, she raised her eyebrows. "In that case, I'm all ears."

CHAPTER THIRTEEN

FAITH REFUSED TO CALL what happened between her and Nick a mistake. But that didn't mean she had to make more out of it than it was, either. Actually, she thought as she leaned her head against the door frame and watched Nick and Austin play catch in her backyard, she didn't know what to make of it. She wanted to enjoy being in a relationship with a kind, funny, sexy man, not spend all of her time worrying about what tomorrow would bring.

For once in her life, she was content with what she had—with who she was—and she wasn't about to let anything spoil that.

She pressed her hands to her warm cheeks as she remembered the things they'd done to each other. How she'd been so aroused simply by the thought of bringing him pleasure.

Before she got married she'd used sex as a way to keep men interested in her. During her marriage it'd been a way to keep ahold of the wealth she'd always longed for. She used to consider herself a sensual woman, one not afraid or embarrassed to use her body to get what she wanted.

But nothing had prepared her for being with Nick.

When he left her house that night, she'd been sated, exhausted and pleasantly sore. And so vulnerable that the moment she'd heard his car pull away, she'd slid to the floor and burst into tears.

Because she'd been so surprised by her response to Nick, she assured herself. She hadn't considered how easy it would be for her to let go. To enjoy being with a man again. That she'd get so wrapped up in Nick, in making love to him, that she'd forget to play a part, and just…be herself. That she'd feel, as if for the first time, she finally knew who she was.

Great sex had a way of messing with your head that way.

But she was afraid it was more than that. It was also Nick. The way he listened when she told him about her past. His easy acceptance of her and Austin, despite her keeping the truth from him, made it almost impossible for her to continue to lie to him.

It also made her realize how desperately she wanted this life, to pretend the past had never happened, that she'd always been Faith Lewis. To do that, she needed to take care of any unfinished business she had as the woman she'd once been. She had to pay her last respects to her mother.

Since Faith and Austin were already on the run when Robin Hawley died of complications from heart disease, Faith hadn't had the chance to say goodbye. This morning she did that the only way she knew how—by buying a headstone for her mother's grave. She couldn't afford much, but the small, flat tombstone she ordered over the

Internet and paid for with money orders was better than continuing to allow her mother's body to lie in an unmarked grave. It was a last sign of respect for the woman who'd raised her the best she knew how.

More importantly, it gave Faith a sense of closure.

Now she opened the screen door and called, "I'm home."

"Hi, Mom," Austin said, not even pausing in his windup.

Nick, wearing a snug white T-shirt and khaki cargo pants, grinned at her from his crouched position, where he caught Austin's pitch. "I promised him ten more pitches and he still has three to go. Is that okay?"

She shrugged as if his smile didn't do funny things to her stomach. Well, what did she expect? This was the first time they were face-to-face since they'd had sex. From her experience, the morning after—or in this case, three days later—was bound to be awkward.

Not that she'd been avoiding him. Even if she'd wanted to see him before now, their schedules hadn't allowed it. She'd worked Saturday and he'd covered a double shift over the weekend.

"While you two finish up," she said, "I'm going to get something to drink."

Nick didn't even rise as he lobbed the ball back to Austin. "We stopped at Brown's Deli after practice and picked up a couple of Italian sandwiches. There's one in the fridge for you if you're hungry."

She slipped off her shoe. "I fed Austin supper before we left."

"I was starving, Mom," Austin claimed. "And Nick says we needed to refill—"

"Refuel," Nick corrected.

Austin nodded so hard, the bill of his ball cap almost touched his chest. "Refuel after such a hard practice. Plus, I'm growing and I need the extra calories. Right, Nick?"

"We worked up a couple of manly appetites tonight," Nick told her with a wink. But the way his eyes skimmed over her knee-length skirt, lingering on her bare legs, made her think he and Austin were talking about two different kinds of hunger.

Damn it. She was so out of her league with him, it took all of her pride not to run inside and hide in a closet.

After taking off her other shoe, she straightened. "Three more pitches and then you need to hit the shower, Austin. And don't you let him talk you into staying out longer," she warned Nick.

"Yes, ma'am," they said in unison, so seriously she was sure they'd done it on purpose.

Inside, she poured herself a glass of sweet iced tea and, after a brief internal debate, pulled out the wrapped sandwich. She and Britney had spent three hours down at the renovated church that now housed Kingsville's local children's performing arts group. They were putting on *Alice in Wonderland* this weekend, and since Britney had volunteered to help with the stage makeup, she'd dragged Faith along. It was a good way to get to know more people in town.

She unwrapped the sandwich, marked the halfway point and cut off a quarter of it. Not that she didn't deserve the entire thing. She did. Especially after getting stuck with a snotty little twelve-year-old who'd insisted her character—the Queen of Hearts—look prettier than Alice, and so made Faith redo her makeup four times. But she wouldn't let the little prima donna irritate her so much that she turned to food for solace.

Besides, what Faith really wanted was chocolate. Preferably fudge. Poured over a vat of mint chocolate-chip ice cream.

Placing her square of sandwich on a small plate, she rewrapped the rest and put it back in the fridge. She'd just removed all traces of olives and taken her first bite when Nick and Austin came inside. A pickle slice slid out and landed with a soft plop on the plate, while oil dripped down her hand.

"You didn't eat it all, did you?" Austin cried, as if she habitually snatched food out of her baby's mouth.

Swallowing, she set the sandwich down and wiped her hand, then her mouth with a paper towel. "Didn't you already eat? Twice?"

"That was, like, five hours ago!"

"I'm sure it seems that way," Faith said. "And since there's plenty left, you may have more. After you've taken a shower."

"Aw, Mom. I want to show Nick my new baseball bat."

"Shower first."

When he looked ready to argue, Nick tapped the brim of Austin's hat, pushing it down so it covered half his face. "I'm not in a hurry. I can stick around long enough for you to wash some of that stink off."

Austin pulled his cap off, his eyes lit up with humor. "At least I don't smell like a girl."

"Who you calling a girl? This is the manliest after-shave they make."

"Sure," her son said between giggles. "If a guy wants to smell like a bunch of flowers."

Nick fake lunged for Austin, who took off shrieking. His laughter faded as he pounded up the stairs.

"What was that all about?" Faith said, nudging the sandwich aside. She wouldn't eat the messy concoction in front of Nick.

Washing his hands at the sink, he glanced at her. "The kids were hassling me at practice because Tracy commented on my aftershave."

Faith's vision took on a red haze. "Oh?"

He dried his hands before hanging her towel back on the rack. "Yep. Seems she wants to buy some for her brother for his birthday."

"I bet she did," Faith mumbled, willing to bet her last paycheck Tracy had used her brother as an excuse so she could sniff at Nick.

"No need to be jealous," he said, with such obvious delight she narrowed her eyes. He laughed. "No need to get pissed at me, either." He bent his head to speak into her ear, his breath sending a shiver up her spine. "I didn't spend the past two days thinking about Tracy, wishing I could be with her. Didn't dream of touching her. Didn't spend hours reliving making love with her."

Faith dropped her gaze and picked an imaginary

piece of lint off her skirt. "I may have thought about you, too. Once or twice."

More like once or twice an hour. And she couldn't even look at her kitchen table and chairs without re-membering how they'd used the one chair for a dry run of his salon chair fantasy.

The sound of water running through the ancient pipes was quickly followed by her new water heater kicking on. "Thank God," Nick said.

Before she could figure out what he was thankful for, he grabbed her hips and crushed his mouth to hers. The kiss was somehow both sweet and hot, and only served to remind her of how far she was falling for Nick.

She'd tried to convince herself she'd told him about her marriage and Austin's abuse out of fear and guilt. It was bound to happen, right? All these years she hadn't been able to count on anyone, to trust anyone. But now…now she had Nick in her life. In her corner.

Tears filled her eyes. She and Austin could stay in Kingsville. They could finally have everything they wanted.

Nick lifted his head, his breath coming out heavy. "I missed you," he said in that simple, honest way of his.

She cleared her throat. "We spoke on the phone every day."

"It's not the same."

"No, I guess not." Although she did enjoy hearing about his day. Hearing his voice. "I missed you, too."

He stepped forward so that his hips pressed her against the counter. "How long a shower does Austin take?"

"I'm lucky if he's in there long enough to get wet. Usually he's in and out within five minutes."

Nick's clear disappointment was almost comical. "That's not quite enough time for what I had in mind," he said, settling his hands on her waist.

Patting his chest, she laughed. "I should hope not. Although you were on the quick side that third time Saturday night…"

He kissed the tip of her nose. "I'll wait until a better time to prove my endurance. Until then…the annual boat show's this weekend down in Rockland and I thought maybe we could go when you're done working Saturday. There are crafts and stuff, and I think Austin would get a kick out of seeing the boats."

"You…you want Austin to go with us?"

"Yeah. And they have these zucchini boat races. Hey, do you think Austin would want to enter that? I bet we could come up with something—"

She threw her arms around him, squeezing tight as she pressed her face into the warmth of his neck.

Nick patted her back. "If I'd known you'd react this way to the mere mention of zucchini boat races I would've brought it up earlier."

She looked up into his wonderful, handsome face. "You don't want to have sex with me—"

"Hey, now, I never said that."

She waved a hand. "You don't *just* want to have sex with me. You want to spend time with me and my son."

"Yes," he said slowly, as if she'd lost her mind.

Using the back of her hand, she brushed her bangs to the side. "I'm just… I can't believe I got this lucky."

He moved his hands up her ribs, his thumbs brushing the undersides of her breasts. "Does any of this mean you want to go to the boat show?"

She pressed against him. Feminine power surged through her when he tensed, his eyes darkening. "That's definitely what it means."

Then she kissed him, hoping to show him how happy he made her feel. How safe.

"You get away from my mom!"

AT AUSTIN'S SHOUT, Faith jumped. Nick stepped back and turned to find the boy standing in the doorway wearing nothing but a pair of knee-length basketball shorts. His hair was damp, his face red, and he held a metal baseball bat over one bare shoulder as if he was about to take a swing. At Nick's head.

Austin stepped into the room, lifting the bat higher. "I said get away from her!"

Faith gasped. "Austin! Put that down right now."

"No. Not until he leaves."

"Honey, Nick wasn't hurting me—"

"He can't touch you like that!" Austin yelled, his voice thick with tears. "It's not right. You shouldn't let him touch you like that."

"How about I just move over here?" Nick asked calmly, keeping his hands in his pockets as he crossed to the table. "Now will you put the bat down?" When Austin continued to glare at him, his grip on the bat so tight his knuckles were white, Nick added quietly, "You're scaring your mom."

"I want to scare *you*," Austin said. "I want you to leave and never come back."

"That's enough," Faith said, her voice shaking. "Austin, apologize to Nick right now and then go to your room. I'll be up shortly."

The boy's expression turned mutinous. "I won't. He should say he's sorry. Not me."

Then he dropped the bat and ran out of the room, the sound of his pounding footsteps up the stairs echoing in the silent house.

"I…I'm so sorry," Faith said, jumping as Austin slammed his bedroom door with a resounding bang. She hugged her arms around herself.

"He's obviously pissed at us, but he's also confused and hurt. Not a good combination in anyone, let alone a kid." Especially a kid with Austin's background. Some victims of sexual abuse suffered mixed-up feelings about sex. And plenty of anger issues to work out, as well. "Give him some time and he'll calm down enough to discuss what happened."

She twisted her fingers together. "I'm not sure what to say to him."

"Do you mind if I talk to him first?" Nick held out a hand when her mouth flattened. "Before you lay into me, rest assured I'm not trying to undermine your authority or take over here."

"No?"

"Listen, it's my fault this happened. I shouldn't have

touched you—not when Austin was home. And I think it's important for him to hear that from me. Just as he should hear it from me that I'm not out to hurt either one of you."

Finally, she nodded. "I'll wait down here."

And that simple statement told him in no uncertain terms that she trusted him.

Outside Austin's bedroom, Nick inhaled deeply, then knocked on the door twice before opening it. Austin was lying on his back crosswise on his bed. Tear tracks stained his cheeks. When he lifted his head to see who'd come in, Nick's chest tightened. He'd seen that same expression on so many of the victims he'd worked with over the years. Anger. Guilt. And way too much pain for a kid to handle alone.

Austin flopped onto his stomach and buried his face in his folded arms.

"I know you're mad at me," Nick said from the doorway, "but I was hoping we could talk. Guy to guy. Can I come in?"

"What if I said no?" Austin asked, his voice muffled.

"Well, since this is your room, I'd have to respect that and walk away. But I'm hoping you'll give me a chance to apologize."

Austin lifted his head. "You're gonna apologize to me?"

"Yeah. I am. If you let me in."

Nick's lungs burned, and it wasn't until Austin gave one of his shrugs that Nick realized he'd been holding his breath, waiting for the answer.

He sat on the bed by Austin's bare feet. "Listen, what you saw, what your mom and I were doing—"

"You were gonna have sex," Austin said flatly.

Nick's head jerked back as if the kid *had* hit him with his bat. "No. We kissed, that's all. Sometimes, when a man and woman…like each other…they kiss." He tugged at the collar of his T-shirt, which seemed to have grown increasingly tight. "You have my word that I'm never going to hurt you or your mom and I'll never do anything to come between you two."

"If you like each other, she should've told me." He laid his cheek on the bedspread, facing away from Nick. "That's why you took me home tonight. That's why you're so nice to me."

Pressing his lips together, Nick tipped his head back. He'd been such an idiot. "Austin, can you look at me?" He waited until the boy grudgingly met his eyes. "Now, I want you to listen carefully. Whatever I feel for your mother has nothing to do with how I feel about you. And the reason I'm nice to you, the reason I spend time with you, is because I think you're one hell of a kid, you got that?"

Austin rolled his eyes and went back to staring at the headboard.

So much for being able to talk his way out of this one. "I'm sorry you found out about your mom and me that way, but I'm not sorry I kissed her. And just because you were upset with us didn't give you the right to talk to your mother how you did downstairs." When Austin remained silent, Nick got to his feet. "I just hope that once you're through being mad, you and I can go back to being friends again."

He walked to the door.

"She shouldn't have let you put your hand there," Austin said faintly.

"What?"

"She shouldn't have let you touch her like that. She should've told you to stop," he said woodenly, as if the words were coming from someone else. "I never told him to stop."

Nick's stomach churned, and cold prickled his skin. "You never told who to stop?"

"My dad," Austin whispered.

Feeling as though his legs were encased in cement, Nick forced himself to go back into the room. To sit once again on the bed. He knew the drill when interviewing a possible victim of sexual abuse. What kind of questions to ask. How to keep his body language unthreatening, his tone calm. How to remain in control no matter what.

But damn, none of those things were easy to do with a child who'd had his innocence brutally taken away.

Though he didn't know if he could handle hearing it, Nick sensed Austin needed someone to talk to. "Do you want to tell me what your dad did to you?"

Tears dripped down the boy's cheeks and onto the bedspread. "He…he touched me. Down there," Austin said, his voice so faint Nick had to strain to hear him. "Made me touch him back." Austin rubbed at his tears, but they still flowed. "He'd come into my room at night after Mommy was sleeping. He said it was our special time. Our special thing."

Nick had never felt so helpless as he did that very

moment. Laying his hand on the boy's head, he brushed back his hair. "Whatever your dad did, it wasn't your fault."

Austin rolled to his side and curled his knees into his chest. "But I didn't want to...do those things. I should've told him no. I should've stopped him. Now we have to move all the time and it's all my fault."

"Bullshit," Nick said vehemently. "You were a little kid and he was the grown-up. Even if you'd tried to stop him, you might not have been able to."

Austin pushed himself to a sitting position, but kept his head down, his hair covering his eyes. "Do you think I'm bad for letting him do those things to me?"

"Absolutely not," Nick said, his hands clenching with impotent rage. He wanted to find Austin's bastard of a father and beat the hell out of him. "Sometimes, when someone is hurt by someone else, they may feel guilty or angry. Or scared. Or all three." He squeezed Austin's shoulder, shocked when the boy rested his head against Nick's side. "Have you ever talked to anyone about what happened?"

He shook his head. "It makes Mom sad."

"That's only because she loves you so much. What about back in New York? Did your mom or maybe a lawyer or police officer take you to talk to someone?"

"I don't remember."

"If you want, I can ask your mom about taking you to see someone who helps kids who have gone through what you've gone through."

"Like you?"

"Sort of. But this wouldn't be a police officer." Austin seemed unsure, so Nick decided to back off. "Tell you what, you think about it and let me know. Now, how about I get your mom? I'm sure she's wondering if we're okay up here."

Before he could get up, though, Austin threw his skinny arms around Nick's waist. "I'm sorry I said those mean things downstairs. I don't want you to go away."

A lump formed in Nick's throat. "We all make mistakes," he said, rubbing Austin's back like his own father used to do to him when he'd been a child and was upset. "And don't you worry. I'm not going anywhere."

Austin looked up at him. "Promise?"

At that moment, Nick would've promised the kid the world. "You have my word. And if you ever need me, if you're in trouble or someone hurts you, or even if you just need someone to talk to, you can come to me. No matter what time, day or night."

Austin snuggled deeper against Nick's side. Kissing the top of his head, Nick wrapped his arm around the boy's slim shoulders. He never wanted to let go.

BY THE TIME FAITH CAME downstairs after tucking a remorseful Austin into bed, she was exhausted. Her baby had felt horrible about how he'd acted.

"He okay?" Nick asked quietly from where he stood at the counter as she came into the kitchen.

She hadn't expected him to stay, but couldn't deny she was glad he had. "He will be. A good night's rest should help." She frowned. "Do I smell coffee?"

Nick moved aside so she could see the half-full pot. "I thought we both could use some."

What she could use was a couple shots of whiskey, but since the only thing in the house containing alcohol was a bottle of mouthwash, coffee would have to do. She took two cups down from the cabinet. After filling them, she handed one to him and then went to the fridge and added milk to hers before sitting at the table.

She took a long sip and sighed. "Thank you," she said, not caring that she sounded pathetically grateful, "for this and for whatever it was you said to Austin to help him calm down."

Leaning back against the counter, Nick crossed his feet at the ankles. "He did most of the talking." He sipped his coffee thoughtfully. "I hope I'm not overstepping here but…have you thought about taking Austin to see a therapist about what his father did to him?"

She jerked, spilling coffee onto her hand and the tabletop. "And have him relive it? No. I…I couldn't do that to him. Besides, I'm not even sure he remembers."

"He remembers."

Her vision swam and she carefully set her cup down. "Did he tell you that?"

Nick nodded shortly, his jaw tight, and her worst fears were confirmed. For so long she'd prayed Austin would be spared those horrible memories…. "Why didn't he ever tell me?" she asked hoarsely.

"I think he's worried it'll upset you."

With her stomach twisting in knots, she snapped,

"Of course it upsets me. But that doesn't mean he can't come to me if he needs me."

"Faith," Nick said gently, "he needs to be able to talk to someone trained to help him recover from being abused."

"I'm helping Austin," she said firmly. "You've seen him these last few weeks. He's coming out of his shell, he has friends and people he can count on. He's learning to trust again." She glanced over at Nick. "And so am I."

He crouched by her chair, resting his hand on her knee. "I can't tell you what it means that you trust me, but I'm worried Austin might need professional help. As a matter of fact, you could both benefit by speaking to a family therapist."

"Just because he had a temper tantrum over seeing something that upset him doesn't mean he needs therapy. But…I'll think about it."

Nick tapped her knee. "And you're saying that to shut me up."

How could he read her so easily? "No. Of course I'm not."

"I have four sisters. Do you think I can't tell when a woman is trying to placate me?"

"I don't want you to shut up. I just…want you to drop this subject. At least until I've had a chance to think things through."

"That's fair enough." Straightening, he finished his coffee and rinsed out his cup before coming back to her. "I'm going to head out, let you get some sleep."

She attempted to smooth her hair. "Do I look that bad?"

"You look beautiful," he said sincerely. "I have to work second shift the next two days, but I'm off Thursday and the Sox are playing a doubleheader that night. How about I bring a couple pizzas over after work and we can all watch the second game?"

"I'm sure he'd love to watch it with you. And so would I."

"I'll see you then." He kissed her forehead, his lips soft and warm and somehow making even that innocent touch seductive. "At least consider the therapist idea. You can't run away from your problems by pretending nothing happened."

She waited until he'd shut the door behind him before crossing her arms on the table and dropping her head on them. Thank God he didn't know her problems weren't the only things she was running from.

CHAPTER FOURTEEN

YOU CAN'T KEEP RUNNING... Making a face at her reflection in the mirror of her workstation, Faith shook her plastic cape out with a snap, then folded it neatly in half.

It wasn't as if she ignored her problems. How could she when they were always there, staring her in the face? She'd do whatever it took to make sure Austin got the help he needed. But she still worried what the help could cost them. Of what could come out if Austin talked to a therapist.

Maybe, in her quest to keep Austin safe, she'd unwittingly made things worse for him, but she'd only been trying to protect him. And hey, her way must not be all wrong, since for the first time in four years she and Austin were part of something bigger than the two of them. They had friends, a community they belonged to and a bright future.

Best of all, they had Nick.

She refilled an empty bottle of de-frizzing cream before double-checking that her curling iron, flatiron and hair dryer were unplugged. Britney had left early to change clothes before her dinner meeting with her newly hired—and seriously cute—accountant. Faith wouldn't be surprised if Harley-riding Michael was soon replaced with horn-rimmed-glasses-wearing Ron.

A definite improvement. She couldn't wait to tell Nick when he came over to watch the ball game tonight.

She smiled at the thought of spending a few hours in front of the TV with him. Instead of fighting her feelings for Nick, she meant to embrace them. Hold on to them for as long as they lasted.

Someone rapped on the door and Faith raised her eyebrows. Obviously the Closed sign she'd flipped over more than ten minutes ago wasn't clear enough. She crossed the room, unlocked and then opened the door.

"Sorry," she told the petite brunette, "we're closed until tomorrow."

The slim woman pouted, her lower lip sticking out slightly. She was young enough, and pretty enough with her big brown eyes, waist-length hair and flowy sundress, that the expression worked on her.

"Maybe I could come in and make an appointment?" she asked, her husky voice at complete odds with her fairy looks. "Since I'm here and all."

Faith hesitated. The shop was closed, but she wasn't in the habit of turning away potential clients. Besides, she really wanted to get her hands on that hair. She was thinking a pixie cut, something short, sharp and edgy, with light caramel and reddish-brown highlights for drama.

Standing aside, she pulled the door open wider. "Come on in and we'll get you set up. Is there a day or time that's better for you?" she asked, walking toward the front desk. She flipped open the appointment book. "I have a ten o'clock on Friday—"

"Actually," the woman said pleasantly, setting her handbag on the counter, "I'm not really here for a haircut."

Faith frowned. "Excuse me?"

Opening her tiny purse, she pulled out a business card.

Faith wasn't sure why, but something told her not to take the card. When she didn't move, the other woman smiled indulgently and set it on the counter. Faith didn't even look at it. Instead, she took a step back.

"My name is Jaiden Leppard, and you," she continued, "are a very hard woman to track down."

Faith swallowed. It felt as if there were a golf ball in her throat. "I don't understand. Do I... Do we know each other?"

"Oh, no. At least, not yet. But as we're going to spend a lot of time together from now on, I suppose that will change. You see, I've been hired to find you—"

Faith's jaw dropped. "You?"

"I can assure you, I'm very good at my job." Jaiden flipped her hair over her shoulder. "Of course, I couldn't have done it if you hadn't purchased that headstone for your mother's grave."

Faith went numb. "I'm not... I don't—"

"You and I both know you did. You shouldn't have parked your car in the Rockport Post Office parking lot. Unless maybe you didn't notice the security cameras?"

Oh, God. Bile rose in her throat and she edged to the side, closer to the shelves of hair products for sale.

She'd thought she was being so clever, using money orders to pay for her mother's headstone. And she'd even gone to several different post offices in Portland to get them, just to be on the safe side.

She'd bought the grave marker to have closure with her past. Instead, that one act had brought her past back with a vengeance.

"I'm sorry," Faith said, hoping the counter blocked Jaiden from seeing that she was reaching behind her. Her hand closed over a bottle of aerosol hair spray. "I think you're confusing me with someone else."

"No, I'm not. As I said, I'm very good at my job. And you, Lynne Addison, aka Faith Lewis, are just who I've been looking for." Then she held up a 4x6 photo.

Try as she might, Faith couldn't stop herself from glancing at it. It was a picture of her and Austin—Jon—posing in front of Yankee Stadium.

Austin was four and she'd taken him to the ballpark to try to coax him out of the angry, sullen mood he'd been in. Not two weeks later, she'd walked in on Miles abusing him.

"Where did you get that?" Faith asked loudly, letting out some of the hysteria she was feeling, to help mask the sound of her flicking the plastic lid off the hair spray bottle.

"From my client—who, by the way, wants you back in New York…. Hey, what are you doing?" Jaiden reached for her bag. "Get your hands where I can—"

Faith leaped forward and sprayed the hair product directly into Jaiden Leppard's eyes.

LESS THAN AN HOUR LATER, Faith opened her front door a few inches.

"Good timing," Nick said as he climbed her porch steps. He held up a pizza box in one hand, a large paper bag in the other. "I just got here."

She knew that. In between packing and loading her car, she'd been watching for him. When he went to step inside, she held on to the door and blocked his way. "Nick, I'm sorry but I—I'm going to have to cancel tonight."

"Everything okay?"

She pressed her lips together as she nodded. "Fi-fine. It's just that…Austin…he's not feeling well—"

"Nick!"

At the sound of her son's distressed cry, she panicked. Before she could stop him, Austin pushed her aside and flew at Nick like a missile.

"Whoa." Nick took a step back to keep his balance while Austin wrapped his arms around his waist. "What's going on, buddy? Your mom says you're sick?"

"I don't want to go." Austin sniffled. His face was wet and puffy, his hair a sweaty mass. "Make her let us stay."

Nick glanced at her in puzzlement. "Why don't we go inside and sit down and you can tell me what's wrong."

"Austin," Faith said, more sharply than she'd intended, her mind scrambling with what to do next, "I told you to stay in your room."

Austin clung to Nick. "I'm not gonna listen to you anymore. You can't make me go."

Her fingers tightened on the door. She had to get Nick out of here. But with Austin still wrapped around him, he nudged her aside and stepped inside. Setting the pizza box down on the empty coffee table, he laid a hand on Austin's head. "Someone want to fill me in?"

Faith shut the door. "This just isn't a good—"

"She's making us leave," Austin said, "but I don't want to move again."

Nick's eyes narrowed. "What?"

"That's enough," Faith warned.

Austin whirled on her. "I don't care if he knows. Nick won't let anyone hurt us."

She grabbed her son by the arm and pulled him away from Nick, holding on when he attempted to yank himself free. "Go to your room. Now."

"I hate you!" Austin claimed, before racing up the stairs.

She hugged her arms around herself and concentrated on breathing, on just getting through the next few minutes. "Well, that, plus you showing up, is the perfect end to this, isn't it?" she said, her voice shaking.

"What did he mean, you're leaving?"

"I really can't get in to—"

"What did he mean?" When she shrugged and tried to open the door, he tossed the bag on top of the pizza box. He stalked toward her, and she pressed her back into the solid wood of the door. Luckily, he stopped a few inches away from her. If he touched her now, she'd break. "Talk to me. What's going on that has you both so upset?"

Her lower lip quivered. She wanted to rest her forehead against his chest. To cling to him like her son had just done. But she couldn't afford to. She'd been such a fool to think she deserved this life.

"We…we're going away. For a few days. There's been… Austin's grandmother is… She's sick and they don't think she has much time…"

"I thought your mother already passed away?"

Had she told him that? Faith was so terrified, so out of control, she couldn't even remember. She pushed away from the door, from the temptation of stepping into his arms. "I meant my grandmother. We're the only family she has left—"

"If you're coming back in a few days," he interrupted quietly, his attention on something behind her, "then where's all your stuff?"

"What stuff?"

"Those pictures of Austin that were here…" He pointed to the long, narrow table that used to hold several framed photos. Striding over to the far end of the couch, he picked up an empty, bright yellow wicker basket. "Austin's comic books used to be in this, and you had a pink-and-white quilt on the back of that chair." When she just stared at him, slack-jawed, he raised his eyebrows. "I'm a cop. It's my job to notice the details."

See why she didn't want him in the house? He was too smart. Too intuitive. And she was too tired and too scared—and cared about him too much—to keep lying. "We're leaving and we're not coming back. And I don't have time to explain more than that."

Unable to face him any longer, she hurried back

upstairs. Austin's door was shut, but she didn't bug him to hurry. Whatever he didn't get packed, they'd have to leave behind. She wanted to be on the road within the next twenty minutes and at least two hundred miles from Kingsville before Jaiden Leppard even realized they were gone.

In her own room, she stuffed a few pairs of jeans and her favorite capri pants into a large rolling suitcase. It wasn't until a drop fell on the back of her hand that she realized she was crying. She didn't have time for the self-indulgence of tears. Besides, she'd been naive to think she and Austin could stay put, that their past wouldn't catch up to them.

Hastily wiping her face, she surveyed the top of her dresser with a practiced eye, grabbing only the necessities: the almost empty bottle of her favorite perfume, the framed handprint Austin had given her for Mother's Day a few years back, and her jewelry box. Her bedroom door slammed against the wall and she whirled around. Nick stood in the doorway, his expression so hard she barely recognized him.

Heart pounding, she schooled her expression and breezed past him to dump the items into the suitcase. "I asked you to go. This is still my house and—"

"You're right, this is your house, so how can you just leave it? Did something happen at work? Did you and Britney get into a fight?"

As much as she hated leaving Britney without a word, that couldn't be helped now. "It's more complicated than that."

Opening her top dresser drawer, she gasped when he yanked her back and slammed it shut, hard enough to make the entire thing shake. "Damn it, what's going on?"

"We have to leave," she told him shakily. "I don't have a choice."

"We all have choices."

She laughed, but the sound was hollow. "Not everyone."

Because he was still in her way, she gave up on emptying her dresser, and instead walked over to her cramped closet. Taking as many items as she could, she folded them over her arm and shoved them into the suitcase, hangers and all. She wondered if there was some way she could squeeze Austin's bike into the trunk. Or maybe tie it on top of the roof?

Grabbing her shoulders, Nick spun her around to face him, his fingers digging into her. "If you're in trouble, tell me so I can help."

"You can't help me!" She threw her arms up to break his hold. "Don't you get that? I'm not some helpless waif who needs a big strong man to protect me. And I'm far from the sweet, innocent woman you want me to be."

His jaw worked as he gritted his teeth. "I don't want you to be anything but who you are."

"That's just it," she cried, using both hands to push him back a step. "You want to know me?" She shoved him again. "Here it is—I'm a liar." The next shove lacked the heat of the first two. "I'm nothing but a liar," she said, her voice breaking. "And as always, those lies are catching up with me. My past is catching up with me."

He reached for her, but she backed away. "Faith—"

"Don't call me that!"

"What?"

"That's not my real name," she said, unable to stand the weight of her deception any longer. "My name, my *real* name, is Lynne Addison. What I told you about my marriage, about what happened to Austin, that was all true, but the rest..." Emotion clogged her throat. "I'm sorry."

He looked dumbstruck. "Why?"

"To protect my son. But it didn't work. He found us. Again."

"Who? Austin's father?"

Nodding, she sank onto the bed and rubbed her burning, gritty eyes. "He hired a private investigator. She wants to take us back to New York. But I can't let Austin return there. I won't."

Nick crouched in front of her. "Let's back up for a minute. Where's this P.I. now?"

A hot flush of shame crept up Faith's neck. "In the salon. When she told me who she was, what she wanted I—I panicked and I locked her in the closet," she finished in a rush.

"You attacked her?" he asked after a long moment.

She twisted her fingers together. "I didn't hurt her. I just sort of...sprayed her in the face with hair spray then...pushed her into the closet. I swear I didn't hurt her—"

"And of course I should believe you because so far you've been so honest, right?"

She winced. "She's fine. But I can't take the

chance of someone finding her before we leave. If Britney goes back to the salon tonight…" Her eyes widened when he took out his cell phone. "What are you doing?"

He shot her a searing look. "I'm calling the station so someone can go check—"

"No!" She leaped at him, managing to take him by surprise and to knock the phone onto the floor. Scrambling after it, she shut it off, clutching it to her chest. "You can't do that. Please, you can't let her send us back."

When he spoke again, his voice was calm. Soothing. "No one's going to make you go back. Even if the P.I. was hired by your ex-husband, I can't believe any court would allow that bastard so much as visitation rights with Austin after being convicted—"

"He was never convicted," she said, her heart pounding so hard she was afraid it would burst out of her chest.

"You told me he went to trial…but you never told me he was convicted, did you?" Nick said thoughtfully, as if recalling their conversation about her past. Raking a hand through his hair, he began to pace, his movements stiff with anger. At the window, he faced her, the setting sun behind him. Shadows played across his face, hiding his expression. "What else didn't you tell me?"

Lowering her arm, she let the cell phone slip out of her sweaty hand and onto the bed. She didn't want to reveal the full extent of her deception, of what she was capable of. But really, what did it matter if he knew the truth now? Even if by some miracle they could stay in Kingsville, there was no way Nick could look past her sins. She'd been such a fool to hope for more than someone like her deserved.

"I didn't tell you so many things," she admitted, forcing herself to meet his eyes.

Though Nick's arms hung loose by his sides, his hands opened and closed. "Does your ex-husband have visitation rights to Austin?"

Knowing what she was about to say would be the end of any feelings Nick might've had for her, she licked her dry lips and forced the truth out in a thin voice. "I don't have an ex-husband. I'm still married."

THE TOP OF NICK'S HEAD tingled, the sensation moving down to his limbs, until his entire body felt frozen. Until he had to lean back against the windowpane just to remain on his feet. He stared at Faith—no, not Faith. What had she said her name was? Lynne. *Sweet God.* He'd made love with her, had cared about her and had started fantasizing about having a life with her and Austin.

And he hadn't even known her real goddamn name.

"You're married? You took your son away from your husband."

She winced. Good. She should wince. She should be scared out of her lying head. "I had to," she said.

He didn't stop her when she crossed to the dresser. He was afraid if he touched her now, when his feelings were so close to the surface, he wouldn't be able to control himself. "Was Austin really abused?"

She scooped up an armful of bras and panties and

tossed them into the suitcase. "You've spoken to him. You know I didn't make that up."

"Maybe you coached him. Told him what to say."

Instead of getting angry, as he'd half hoped, she zipped up the suitcase and, using both hands, slid it to the floor. "I didn't. But I don't blame you for wondering."

He sneered. "Well, hell. Thanks for being so understanding."

She ducked her head, her hair covering her face. Pushing away from the window, he stalked the length of the bed. Tried to keep his cool, to keep his riotous emotions in check. She continued packing as if she hadn't just dropped a bomb on him. What clothes didn't fit in the suitcase were shoved into a large duffel bag. Shoes were tossed into plastic grocery bags and set by the door. She didn't even glance at the paperbacks lining the small bookcase or the knickknacks on the nightstand.

"This isn't the first time you've had to cut and run with little notice," he said slowly.

Reaching under her mattress, she didn't even glance up at him. "No."

"And you never told the police Austin was abused…"

She pulled her hand out, and with it, a thick business envelope stuffed with money. "I wanted to. I wanted him to pay for what he did to Austin but… Miles, my husband, *was* brought up on charges of abusing a child. He molested a boy who attended the after-school program he'd set up for underprivileged youths, but there wasn't enough evidence to convict him."

"So you just let him get away with it?"

Her eyes flashed. "You're a cop. You should know better than anyone that even if I had told the police what Miles did to Austin, there's no guarantee he'd be sent to prison. And after he was acquitted in his trial he was so…smug. As if nothing could touch him. And he was right. That's when I knew if I wanted to get Austin away from him, I had to do something drastic."

"I'd say kidnapping your own child is as drastic as you could get."

She yanked the zipper of the duffel bag closed. "It's not kidnapping. He's my son. *Mine.*"

"Why didn't you tell the prosecution about Austin's abuse? That could've been enough to help them get a conviction."

"Don't you think I get that?" she asked, throwing the bag on the floor. "I've lived with that decision every day. Do you have any idea what I'd give if I could go back and do it all over again? How many things I'd do differently? I was just…" She pulled her hair back from her face with both hands. "God, I was terrified. The night I found out what he was doing to Austin, I tried to leave, but Miles warned me if I so much as stepped outside without his permission, he'd have me arrested for taking his son. That no judge would grant me custody of Austin over him. Not with my background."

Faith had the same defeated tone he'd heard all too often in victims. "You could've gone to the police—"

"He said they wouldn't believe me. That they'd see me as a vengeful, gold-digging whore," she snapped. "And since that wasn't far from the truth at the time, I believed him. He warned me that if I filed for divorce, he'd get Austin. He had everything I didn't," she continued, ticking the list off on her fingers. "Wealth, connections, a spotless reputation. I had nothing. All the credit cards were in his name, all the bank accounts. So I stayed. But from that night on, I never left Austin alone with his father. I even slept in his room to make sure Miles couldn't get to him. And I prayed that somehow, someday, we'd be able to get away."

Nick tried to hold on to his anger, but realizing what she'd gone through, hearing the real fear in her voice, didn't make it easy. Not when all she wanted was to protect her child. "How did you and Austin escape him?"

"After his acquittal, Miles threw a party for all the people who'd supported him during the trial. I'd been so hopeful he'd be sent to prison, and was so crushed when he was found not guilty, I…I had too much to drink and I accused the head of his defense team of helping a monster go free."

"What did he say?"

"She. Allison Martin. Miles interrupted us before I could say much more than that, but then…then Allison called me. As much as she hated to think she'd had a part in setting a pedophile free, she'd done some digging into Miles's background and what she found convinced her I was telling the truth. Unfortunately, she knew it wasn't strong enough to convince the D.A. to bring up new charges against Miles."

"So this Allison helped you escape."

"She felt so guilty…we came up with a plan, and

one day Lynne and Jon Addison just…disappeared. Allie gave us enough money to get by until we could get settled somewhere. We'd even hoped we could stay in Serenity Springs, her hometown. That we could start a new life there." Faith pressed the heels of her hands to her eyes. "But that'll never happen. We'll never be free of Miles."

Serenity Springs. No wonder Austin had been so freaked out when he'd let it slipped they'd lived there. And then, when Nick had asked Faith about it, she'd said it was a town called Serenity Hills. Another one of her many lies.

"Are you going to spend your entire life running?" He strode over to her, too pissed to care that she backed up, her hand at her throat, her eyes wide. "You can fight him now. You have a decent job. Friends. Damn it, Faith, you have me. We can fight him together. Once Austin tells the police what his father did—"

"There's no way I'm letting my baby live through it again. I saw what that other boy went through. He came forward and had to relive every detail in court, only to be made to look like a liar. And afterwards he—he took his grandmother's sewing scissors and slit his wrists," Faith said hoarsely. "He was only eleven years old. He survived, but I have no idea what's happened to him since."

Nick burned at what that poor kid must've gone through. "It'll be hard for Austin, but he lives with it every day. He needs to know his father is being punished. He needs to heal."

"And what if we fail?" she cried. "What if Austin has to live with Miles? I can't take that chance."

"I'll keep you and Austin safe."

"That's not your job."

He grabbed her by the upper arms and lifted her onto her bare toes. "The hell it isn't! I love you!"

Her head snapped back as if he'd sucker punched her. He felt as if he'd just taken one to the chin himself. He hadn't meant to let that slip. Hadn't wanted to admit, even to himself, how much he'd fallen for her and her kid.

And he'd thought she looked scared before. "You… you can't love me," she said in a desperate whisper. "Faith Lewis isn't even real."

He gritted his teeth instead of shaking her as he wanted to. "You think I'm happy about this? You've lied to me and my family from the minute you stepped into town, and yet, real or not, I love you. I want you and Austin in my life."

Her eyes welled with tears. "I'm sorry."

He let go of her. "You're sorry? That's the best you can do?"

"I can't stay—"

"You mean you won't. Because it's easier to run and be on your own than ask for help. You'd rather have your pride than build a real life in a place where you can belong."

She looked stricken. "Even if Miles was charged with abusing Austin, I can't put my son through the trauma of a trial." Picking up her duffel bag, she adjusted the strap over her shoulder, then took the handle of the suitcase in a white-knuckled grip. "I've made too many mistakes already. Doing things by the book doesn't work with Miles. He's a master at manipulation and getting what he wants. He's already gotten away with his abuse for years, and there's nothing I can do to change that."

"Only because you're too scared to try."

"Yes, I'm scared. Is that what you want to hear? I'm terrified of losing my son."

There was only one way to force her to stay. To force her to accept his help. "I could place you under arrest," he said quietly.

She paled. "You'd… Would you really do that?"

He wanted to. It scared the hell out of him how much he'd love nothing more than to take her and Austin to the station, where he could protect them. For the first time in his life, that thin line between right and wrong that he always used as his guide disappeared, and he wasn't sure where to stand.

He was pissed, and hurt enough to want to make Faith face her past, to let him help her. But he loved her and Austin enough to let them go.

"I need to let the private eye out of the closet," he said. "The way I figure it, you've got less than twenty minutes to get out of town."

She shut her eyes briefly with a soft exhalation. "Thank—"

"Don't even think about thanking me," he said harshly, curling his fingers into his palms. "Just go."

Then he did the hardest thing he'd ever done in his life. He walked away.

CHAPTER FIFTEEN

DRY-EYED AND BEYOND exhausted, Faith sat in a lumpy chair in front of the motel room window. Using a pen she'd dug out of her purse, she moved the dusty drapes aside just enough to sneak a peek at the parking lot, squinting against the rising sun. The same two cars that had been there when she and Austin arrived at the roadside motel three hours ago were still parked outside. No one had followed them. Yet.

She let the drapes fall back in place and set her pen down on the scarred, round table. Shrugging her shoulders to try to ease some of the aching tension, she got to her feet. As she rolled her head from side to side, she glanced at Austin, asleep on the bed. After they'd left Kingsville, she'd headed north, sticking as close to the coast as possible. When the fog had moved in, she'd realized she should've gone farther inland, but as usual when she made a mistake, she didn't try to correct it. Just made the best of it.

And that's what she would continue to do, she thought as she began to pace across the stained, matted carpet. So this motel wasn't fancy—or clean. They'd be here only a few more hours. Long enough for them both to get some rest. Then they'd be on their way.

Too bad she had no idea where they were going.

Her stomach cramped as she thought about starting over again. She had no one to help her, no one she could trust. Plus she'd spent the bulk of her savings on the headstone for her mother's grave. Five hundred dollars wouldn't get her far. How was she supposed to keep Austin fed and clothed and safe now?

Unbidden memories assaulted her. Austin's laughter as he and Trevor jumped into the pool on the Fourth of July. The warmth of Nick's family at their picnic. How she and Britney always sang along when "Lady Marmalade" played on the radio at the salon.

The way Nick had looked at her when they'd made love. The feel of him inside her. How she'd never felt more…complete.

Wherever she and Austin ended up, she'd be smarter this time. More careful. Like she used to be. No trying to fit into a town. No making friends. And above all, no getting involved with anyone, especially some too-good-to-be-true cop.

No falling in love.

Her pulse raced. She didn't love Nick. Yes, she cared about him and she appreciated him letting her and Austin go, when by all rights, he should've arrested her. But just because he was handsome and honest and wonderful with her son didn't mean she was in love with him.

Flipping on the light in the tiny bathroom, she recoiled at the sight of the dirt-encrusted sink. There were no disposable cups, just a tall drinking glass with the remnants of someone else's lipstick. She shut her eyes and tipped her head back. It was only for one night.

Opening her eyes, she leaned over the sink, studying her reflection in the fuzzy mirror. She was pale, her hair scraped back in a ponytail, her eyes bleak. She looked like hell, which was fitting, considering that's how she felt. Straightening, she pushed herself back from the sink and about jumped out of her skin when the biggest, ugliest bug she'd ever seen skittered across the faucet.

With a shriek, she flew out of the bathroom, slamming the door behind her before jumping onto the bed. Austin didn't even stir as she slid as close to him as possible. He'd fallen asleep about thirty miles before they'd arrived, and once she'd seen how disgusting the room was, she hadn't brought him in until she'd laid the pink-and-white quilt from home on the bed.

No. Not home. It was just a house. A place where they'd felt safe for a while. But it wasn't home. They'd never have a home. This was their life—moving from town to town. Keeping their distance. Never having a place to call their own.

Oh, God. What had she done? Faith moaned and rocked back and forth, sobs racking her body.

Tears ran down her cheeks. She'd taken away any chance Austin had of a normal, healthy life. Nick was right—she did run from her problems, and she would always be running if she didn't make a change. Take a chance. For once fight for what she wanted. Austin was worth the risk. So was Nick.

And by God, so was she.

She wasn't the person she used to be, or the woman Miles accused her of being. She hadn't used Nick. She loved him.

Inhaling raggedly, she grabbed for her purse on the nightstand, reaching into it for a tissue. After drying her face and blowing her nose, she slid the bag onto her shoulder, tucked the quilt's edges around Austin and picked him up. She staggered under his weight and he lifted his head.

"Mom?" he asked, his eyes still closed.

"Shh…" She kissed his cheek. "Go back to sleep. Everything's okay."

"Where're we going?"

Bending slightly so she could unlock the door, she yanked it open and stepped out into the brilliant, sunny morning. "We're going home."

NICK STARED BLINDLY at the ball game on his TV as he finished his bottle of beer. Picking up half of the ham-and-Swiss sandwich he'd made for supper, he brought it to his mouth, but couldn't make himself take a bite. He dropped it back onto the paper plate and opened another beer.

Someone knocked at his front door and he sighed. Debated about whether or not to even bother answering the damn thing. If it was one of his sisters—or worse, his mother—he was faking an intestinal illness. All five of them had already called him—at least once each—to check up on him. He didn't think he could deal with any of them, or their sympathy, in person today.

He'd spent a long, hellish night thinking about Faith and Austin, wondering where they were, if they were safe. What he could've done or said differently to get them to stay. Then, around nine this morning, he'd gotten a frantic call from Britney. She'd been in a panic over Faith not showing up for work or answering her phone.

He'd hated lying to his sister, hated pretending he didn't know what had happened to them. So he'd simply told her he was sure they were fine then promised to check on their house. When he got there, he'd actually been disappointed to find it empty. As if Faith might have somehow changed her mind… Just proved how gullible he really was. Frowning, he took another sip of beer. He wanted to wing the bottle at his expensive TV.

Another knock, this one more insistent, made him slam his bottle on the table with such force that foam spilled over the top. He got to his feet. Hell, couldn't a man even brood in peace?

"What?" he growled, opening the door.

"We're back!" Austin cried, and then launched himself into Nick's arms.

Stunned, Nick couldn't do more than react, his arms automatically going around the boy and pulling him close. It was only after a moment or two that he realized what was happening, and he tightened his hold.

Austin was here. More importantly, he was safe. Nick closed his eyes and buried his face in the boy's hair. The kid had smelled better, but at this point Nick would take him any way he could get him.

Letting go, somehow knowing Nick would never let

him fall, Austin leaned back, his arms outstretched. "I told you he'd be happy to see us."

Nick's brain started working again and he looked up, his heart doing one slow roll when he met Faith's eyes. "Is everything okay?" he asked, as Austin clutched his shirt and pulled himself back up. "Are you all right?"

Faith opened her mouth, but Nick, quickly looking up and down his street, yanked her inside, shutting the door behind her. He didn't agree with the choices she had made, but he wasn't about to let them get sent back to her bastard of a husband.

"We're fine," she assured him. She patted his hand, and that's when he realized he had a viselike grip on her arm. He let go, but noticed he left finger marks on her delicate skin.

"Sorry," he mumbled, setting her son on his feet.

"Can I use your bathroom?" Austin asked. "I really gotta pee."

"First door on the right." He'd barely gotten the last word out before Austin took off like a shot.

Nick studied Faith's face, wanting to memorize every feature. Dark circles rimmed her eyes, and her hair was frizzy and pulled back in a sloppy ponytail. She wore the same clothes she'd had on last night, but her shirt was wrinkled, and if he wasn't mistaken, that was a coffee stain on her pants.

She was the most beautiful thing he'd ever seen.

He turned and walked over to the couch. Picked up the remote and muted the TV before facing her again.

"What are you doing here, Faith? Did something happen? Did that P.I. find you?"

"What happened when you got there? I didn't hurt her, did I?" she countered.

He'd been half-afraid he was going to find the P.I. bloody and bruised. Though he couldn't imagine Faith hurting someone, she'd been desperate. And desperate people were dangerous people.

"Her eyes were red and swollen, but other than that—and being mighty pissed off—she was fine. Actually, she was fine enough that she ripped me up one side and down the other for helping you get away. Even threatened to bring what she called my 'illegal activities' to my captain's attention."

Faith's eyes widened. "Can she do that?"

"Make threats and accusations?" He shrugged. "Sure. I tried telling her I'd just happened to stop by to get some paperwork I'd promised Britney I'd take care of, but she already knew we were…involved. Luckily, she was more interested in picking up your trail than filing charges against you for assault, or for going after me."

That, and the fact that Britney had no idea a woman had been locked in her closet for over an hour, were the only bright spots to an unbelievably shitty night.

"I'm so sorry I got you involved in all of this."

"I made a choice."

"And you chose to protect us."

"A lot of good it did me," he said flatly. "You still left."

"I made a mistake," she said in a breathless rush.

"Really?" He forced his voice to remain cool, viciously tamping out the hope that tried to ignite. "And what would that be?"

Chewing on her thumbnail, she stepped toward him, her eyes beseeching. Then she dropped her hand to her side. "I need…" She swallowed. "I was hoping… I want another chance."

"You left!" he exclaimed, his control snapping. Glancing behind him to make sure Austin hadn't come back, Nick lowered his voice. "I told you I loved you, but that wasn't enough. And now you've, what… changed your mind?"

She pulled her shoulders back. "Yes."

"Is this another game?" Nick murmured. "Because I can't—"

"It's not a game. I thought I had to leave, that I had no other choice. We made it as far as some town called Woodland, and I was trying to figure out my next move when I realized I didn't want to run. Not anymore." Faith reached for him, her hand trembling when he stepped back. "I want to stand up to Miles. I'm willing to fight for the life I want. The life I want with you," she added softly. "But I…I can't do it alone. I need you, Nick."

Her words slammed into him. "You need me? I tried to help you, but you threw it back in my face. You didn't trust me enough, and now, all of the sudden, you do?" He shook his head. "How do I know you won't take off again?"

"Can I have some of those chips?" Austin asked as he came back into the room and zeroed in on the bag Nick had opened to have with his sandwich. "I'm starved."

"Sure, buddy," Nick managed to say. "Help yourself.

You can have that sandwich, too, if you want it. I'm going to talk to your mom in the kitchen, okay?"

Austin, already entranced by the game on TV, nodded absently and, plopping down on the sofa, shoved his hand into the chip bag. Nick gripped Faith's elbow and steered her to the kitchen.

Once there, he raked his hand through his hair. "Look, I don't know if I can do this. You lied to me…to my family. Hell, Britney's a wreck. She was ready to call out the National Guard until I convinced her you must've left of your own free will, considering there was no evidence of foul play and your clothes were gone. Even then she stuck up for you. Told me that you and she were friends, and she knew you wouldn't just take off like that without telling her. She loves you, she considered you a friend, and you used her. You used all of us."

Tears filled Faith's eyes, but he hardened his heart against them. "Yes, I did. I was wrong. So wrong. And I…I don't blame you for not trusting me. I called Allison Martin and asked for her help one more time."

"Allison Martin—the woman who got you out of New York?"

"Yes. I haven't had any contact with her since we left Serenity Springs, but luckily, I was able to get her new cell phone number."

Faith looked so beat, he pulled a chair out and gestured for her to sit. She shook her head.

"Allie lives in Dallas now, but she agreed to meet me in New York tomorrow morning and act as my legal counsel. I'm going to turn myself in." Though her voice shook, Faith's gaze never wavered. "And I want... I was hoping you'd go with me when I do."

His throat constricted. As much as he wanted her back, Nick didn't want her to end up in jail—or worse, lose Austin to that monster she'd married. Both of which were very real possibilities. And though her facing her husband was the right thing to do, Nick had to make sure she understood the consequences. "What you're doing is a risk. You could be charged—"

"I know what I'm doing. The chance I'm taking. Which is why before I do, I need to know Austin will be safe. That no matter what happens to me, he won't be sent back to Miles." Faith closed the distance between them and laid her hand on his chest. "And the only person I trust my son with...is you."

Humbled, Nick could only nod. "I'll keep him safe. I promise."

"And maybe...once this is done...maybe you could learn to forgive me. The only reason I'm strong enough to do this is because of you. Because of your belief in me. Being with you, trusting you, will never be a mistake. And I want to show you that you can trust me, too. With everything." She looked up at him, and what he saw in her eyes made his heart race. "I love you, Nick."

He shut his eyes. How the hell was he supposed to fight his feelings for her when she hit him with such simple honesty?

He pressed his forehead against hers. "I love you, too, Faith. Always. What happens next won't be easy, but together, we're strong enough to face it." He leaned back so he could meet her eyes. "We'll get through this. Don't you ever doubt that."

"I won't." She pressed her lips against his in a kiss filled with love and promise. "I'll be okay as long I have you by my side."

"You've got me," he told her, pulling her close. "Forever."

EPILOGUE

Six months later

NICK PULLED TO A STOP in front of Andrea's house and shut off the ignition. Snow fell softly from the January sky, covering the driveway and the row of cars with a dusting of white.

"I thought you said this was going to be a quiet family dinner," Faith said.

"Those cars do belong to family," Nick insisted. "Well, family and Ethan and Lauren. And if I'm not mistaken, that's Kathleen's new boyfriend's Jeep." He reached over to play with a strand of Faith's hair. "But if you're not up for it, I'll be more than happy to just go home, where we can have a private homecoming celebration."

Faith's heart leaped. *Home.* For the first time, she and Austin had a place they belonged, people they belonged with. She glanced into the backseat, but Austin was still sound asleep, his head against the door, his mouth open.

"You're not getting off that easily." She kissed Nick's palm before unbuckling her seat belt. "And if you think I'm going to leave without eating first, you're nuts.

Britney said your mom made lasagna, and I want some. So let's get inside. I'm starving."

He seemed to hesitate, but so briefly, she wondered if she'd imagined it. "You want me to carry Austin inside?"

"No, I'll wake him."

Nick pulled on his earlobe. "Okay, but just…just hold tight for a minute, would you?"

"What do you mean?"

"I need you to wait. Just…wait right there."

She frowned and zipped up her coat. It was amazing how quickly a car could lose its heat when it was twenty degrees outside. "What am I waiting for?"

"You'll find that out soon enough," he said, then got out and slammed the door.

Shaking her head, she shifted and turned to waken Austin, but then noticed Nick pacing behind the car. Was he… She narrowed her eyes, craning her neck to see… Was he talking to himself?

Maybe the stress of everything that had happened was finally catching up to him. He'd been nothing but rock solid from the moment he'd driven her and Austin down to New York so she could turn herself in to the NYPD. He'd even wanted to take a leave of absence from the Kingsville P.D. to stay with them in New York, since she wasn't allowed to leave the city. But she'd refused to let him make that sacrifice. Instead, he'd driven down every day off he had, and they'd talked on the phone several times a day.

Faith wasn't sure she could've gotten through the past six months without his love and support. Plus, she'd had Allie on her side. The attorney had flown in several times, representing Faith, until two months ago when she'd had to hand her case over to a trusted friend and ex-colleague. Something she wouldn't have done if she hadn't been eight-and-a-half months pregnant and unable to travel.

Wrinkling her nose, Faith watched Nick continue his pacing. Yeah, he was definitely talking to himself, and was even adding hand gestures, which went beyond strange. He must be more tired than she realized.

She shook Austin's shoulder. "Wake up, honey. We're in Kingsville. We're home."

He groaned and shrugged away from her, curling toward the door. Poor kid. She almost hated to waken him, since this was the soundest he'd slept since they'd left Kingsville. Their time in New York had taken a physical, mental and emotional toll on all three of them. And there'd been times when Faith wasn't sure she could go through with facing her past—especially when Miles was granted weekly supervised visits with Austin.

But they'd come through. Together.

Since she and Miles were still legally married and didn't have a custody agreement, she'd been charged with custodial interference instead of kidnapping. In the deal she'd made with the district attorney's office, she'd pleaded guilty, and been sentenced to three years probation. In exchange for her plea, she'd agreed to testify against Miles—and had allowed Austin to testify, as well.

Miles had been charged with sexually abusing their

son. Once the story of his new arrest got around, the son of one of his business associates came forward to admit he'd been abused by Miles, as well. During the trial, the evidence against him was overwhelming. So much so that even Miles's secretary couldn't defend her loyalty to him any longer. Sondra admitted that during the first investigation, Miles had her hide his laptop at her sister's house. A laptop she handed over to the police. Between the boys' powerful testimonies and the child pornography on Miles's laptop, the jury had needed only a few hours to reach a verdict. A verdict they'd delivered just that afternoon.

Guilty. On all charges.

The district attorney felt confident the judge would impose the maximum sentence, and while Faith had to return to court next month to try and get her own ruling overturned, she, Nick and Austin hadn't wasted any time. They'd gone back to the tiny walk-up where Faith and Austin had been living, packed their belongings and headed home.

The car door opened and she turned, the frigid air hitting her face like a slap. "I can't…" She gaped at Nick, her heart picking up speed. "What are you doing?"

Nick, one bended knee down in the snow, held out a closed ring box and scowled. "Shh…"

She raised her eyebrows. "Did you just shush me?"

"Quiet," he said irritably. "If you keep talking, I'll never be able to remember what I'm supposed to say."

"Sorry," she said, before pressing her lips together to squelch a smile.

"Okay. So…" He shook snow off his head. "The thing is…I love you—"

"Oh, Nick," Faith cried, her heart about bursting, "I love you, too."

He sent her a dark look. She mimed zipping her lips together.

"Like I said, I love you and I love Austin—as if he's my own. I want to spend the rest of my life with you both, and I want us to be a family. I want to be there for you in good times and bad. And I promise, if you'll agree to be my wife, if you'll agree to share your son with me, that I'll do everything in my power to protect you, cherish you and love you. Both of you," he said huskily. Inhaling a ragged breath, Nick lifted the lid of the ring box. "Faith Lewis, will you marry me?"

The ring, a white-gold band with an emerald-cut diamond in the center, was simple, and so perfect she forgot to breathe. Faith blinked away tears, causing them to streak down her cheeks.

"You stood by me," she said, then cleared her throat. "You forgave me and you made me see how strong I can be. But most important, you saw the real me and you loved me." Leaning forward, she touched her lips to his, then straightened to look into his eyes. "Yes. I'll definitely marry you."

He shut his eyes briefly, as if in relief, then cupped one hand behind her head and pulled her down for another kiss.

Faith wasn't sure how much time passed as their kiss grew heated, but by the time Austin stretched and yawned in the backseat, both she and Nick were breathing hard.

"What's going on?" Austin asked sleepily as he shimmied his thin frame in between the front seats and plopped onto the driver's side.

"Great news, buddy," Nick said. "We're getting married."

Austin's eyes widened. He grinned. "Yeah? Me, too?"

"Of course you, too," Nick assured him. "We're going to be a family."

With a whoop, Austin launched himself across his mom and into Nick's arms, his knee digging into Faith's stomach. "Ow," she said, laughing through her tears. "Watch those bony knees."

Nick stood, taking Austin with him. "Here," he said, passing her the ring. "See if it fits."

Her hands trembled so violently she wasn't sure she could even put it on. But she managed to get it out of the box and onto her finger without dropping it. She held her hand up to the dome light. "Perfect fit."

"That we are," Nick said.

Faith got out of the car and took his hand. Then, with the man she loved still holding her son, they trudged up the snow-covered walk to start their new life together.

* * * * *

Harlequin offers a romance for every mood!
See below for a sneak peek from our
suspense romance line
Silhouette® Romantic Suspense.
Introducing HER HERO IN HIDING by
New York Times *bestselling author Rachel Lee.*

Kay Young returned to woozy consciousness to find that she was lying on a soft sofa beneath a heap of quilts near a cheerfully burning fire. When she tried to move, however, everything hurt, and she groaned.

At once she heard a sound, then a stranger with a hard, harsh face was squatting beside her. "Shh," he said softly. "You're safe here. I promise."

"I have to go," she said weakly, struggling against pain. "He'll find me. He can't find me."

"Easy, lady," he said quietly. "You're hurt. No one's going to find you here."

"He will," she said desperately, terror clutching at her insides. "He always finds me!"

"Easy," he said again. "There's a blizzard outside. No one's getting here tonight, not even the doctor. I know, because I tried."

"Doctor? I don't need a doctor! I've got to get away."

"There's nowhere to go tonight," he said levelly. "And if I thought you could stand, I'd take you to a window and show you."

But even as she tried once more to pull away the quilts, she remembered something else: this man had been gentle when he'd found her beside the road, even when she had kicked and clawed. He hadn't hurt her.

Terror receded just a bit. She looked at him and detected signs of true concern there.

The terror eased another notch and she let her head sag on the pillow. "He always finds me," she whispered.

"Not here. Not tonight. That much I can guarantee."

*Will Kay's mysterious rescuer protect her
from her worst fears?
Find out in HER HERO IN HIDING by*
New York Times *bestselling author Rachel Lee.
Available June 2010,
only from Silhouette® Romantic Suspense.*

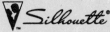

ROMANTIC
SUSPENSE

Sparked by Danger, Fueled by Passion.

NEW YORK TIMES AND *USA TODAY*
BESTSELLING AUTHOR

RACHEL LEE

BRINGS YOU AN ALL-NEW
CONARD COUNTY: THE NEXT GENERATION SAGA!

Conard County THE NEXT GENERATION

After finding the injured Kay Young on a deserted country
road Clint Ardmore learns that she is not only being hunted
by a serial killer, but is also three months pregnant.
He is determined to protect them—even if it means
forgoing the solitude that he has come to appreciate.
But will Clint grow fond of having an attractive woman
occupy his otherwise empty ranch?

Find out in

Her Hero in Hiding

Available June 2010 wherever books are sold.

Visit Silhouette Books at www.eHarlequin.com

Love Inspired®

Bestselling author

JILLIAN HART

brings you another heartwarming story
from

the

GRANGER
FAMILY
RANCH

Rancher Justin Granger hasn't seen his high school sweetheart
since she rode out of town with his heart. Now she's back, with
sadness in her eyes, seeking a job as his cook and housekeeper.
He agrees but is determined to avoid her...until he discovers
that her big dream has always been him!

The Rancher's Promise

*Available June
wherever books are sold.*

Steeple
Hill®

LI87601

www.SteepleHill.com

REQUEST YOUR FREE BOOKS!

2 FREE NOVELS PLUS 2 FREE GIFTS!

◆ HARLEQUIN®

Super Romance®

Exciting, emotional, unexpected!

YES! Please send me 2 FREE Harlequin® Superromance® novels and my 2 FREE gifts (gifts are worth about $10). After receiving them, if I don't wish to receive any more books, I can return the shipping statement marked "cancel." If I don't cancel, I will receive 6 brand-new novels every month and be billed just $4.69 per book in the U.S. or $5.24 per book in Canada. That's a saving of at least 15% off the cover price! It's quite a bargain! Shipping and handling is just 50¢ per book.* I understand that accepting the 2 free books and gifts places me under no obligation to buy anything. I can always return a shipment and cancel at any time. Even if I never buy another book from Harlequin, the two free books and gifts are mine to keep forever.

135/336 HDN E5P4

Name _____ (PLEASE PRINT) _____

Address _____ Apt. #

City _____ State/Prov. _____ Zip/Postal Code

Signature (if under 18, a parent or guardian must sign) _____

Mail to the **Harlequin Reader Service:**
IN U.S.A.: P.O. Box 1867, Buffalo, NY 14240-1867
IN CANADA: P.O. Box 609, Fort Erie, Ontario L2A 5X3

Not valid for current subscribers to Harlequin Superromance books.

**Are you a current subscriber to Harlequin Superromance books
and want to receive the larger-print edition?
Call 1-800-873-8635 today!**

* Terms and prices subject to change without notice. Prices do not include applicable taxes. N.Y. residents add applicable sales tax. Canadian residents will be charged applicable provincial taxes and GST. Offer not valid in Quebec. This offer is limited to one order per household. All orders subject to approval. Credit or debit balances in a customer's account(s) may be offset by any other outstanding balance owed by or to the customer. Please allow 4 to 6 weeks for delivery. Offer available while quantities last.

Your Privacy: Harlequin Books is committed to protecting your privacy. Our Privacy Policy is available online at www.eHarlequin.com or upon request from the Reader Service. From time to time we make our lists of customers available to reputable third parties who may have a product or service of interest to you. If you would prefer we not share your name and address, please check here. ☐

Help us get it right—We strive for accurate, respectful and relevant communications. To clarify or modify your communication preferences, visit us at www.ReaderService.com/consumerschoice.

HSR10R